Undone Business

A Pride and Prejudice Novella Variation

Rose Fairbanks

Undone Business

Rose Fairbanks

Published by Rose Fairbanks

©2015 Rose Fairbanks

Several passages in this novel are paraphrased from the works of Jane Austen.

Cover image by Peculiar World Designs.

ISBN-13: 978-1508731726

ISBN-10: 1508731721

" ...and yet what is there so very laudable in a precipitance which must leave very necessary business undone..."

~ Jane Austen
Pride and Prejudice, Chapter 10

Chapter 1

November 26, 1811

Netherfield looked as opulent as any house from the ton, adorned in flowers from the conservatory. The couples around them laughed and conversed. Despite the general gaiety of the evening, Fitzwilliam Darcy and Elizabeth Bennet remained silent as they went down the dance. At long last, Mr. Darcy asked his partner, "Do you and your sisters often walk to Meryton?" They turned about each other.

"Yes, nearly daily." She paused and raised her eyebrows. "When you met us there the other day, we had just been forming a new acquaintance."

Immediately, Darcy felt his body tense as he fought to keep his face from turning red in anger. He glared at Elizabeth. "Mr. Wickham is blessed with such happy manners as may ensure his making friends—whether he may be equally capable of retaining them, is less certain."

"He has been so unlucky as to lose your friendship," replied Elizabeth, "and in a manner which he is likely to suffer from all his life."

His irritation redoubled as he realized Wickham had actually found opportunity sometime in the last rain-soaked week to speak to her. Darcy imagined Wickham sitting beside her, inhaling her tantalizing rosewater scent, and smiling charmingly while putting her at ease. His lies of woe likely played on Elizabeth's tender heart, but Darcy could say or do nothing without possibly exposing his sister. He tried to change the subject.

"What think you of books?"

Elizabeth refused to consider the topic and instead returned to Wickham. "You are careful in the creation of your implacable resentment, are you not?"

"I am," he said in a firm voice. How could she believe Wickham?

"And never allow yourself to be blinded by prejudice?"

"I hope not."

"It is particularly incumbent on those who never change their opinion, to be secure of judging properly at first."

"May I ask to what these questions tend?"

"Merely to the illustration of your character. I am trying to make it out."

"And what is your success?"

She shook her head. "I do not get on at all. I hear such different accounts of you as puzzle me exceedingly."

"I can readily believe," answered he gravely, "that reports may vary greatly with respect to me, and I could wish, Miss Bennet, that you were not to sketch my character at the present moment, as there is reason to fear that the performance would reflect no credit on either."

"But if I do not take your likeness now, I may never have another opportunity."

"I would by no means suspend any pleasure of yours," he coldly replied.

She said no more, and they went down the other dance and parted in silence. He wished to be angry at Elizabeth but found all of it centred on Wickham. How had he targeted her? She was the one person who could tempt him to explain his history with Wickham. He resolved to find a way to warn her without exposing Georgiana. He hoped, rather than believed, he only desired to protect her instead of improve her opinion of him.

November 30, 1811

Darcy sat at the breakfast table in Netherfield and struggled to read his letter from Bingley once more.

"Mr. Darcy, what does Charles say?" Miss Bingley asked. She leaned to one side to see around the tall floral arrangement she had designed.

"He says his business in town is taking longer than expected, but he hopes to return within a few more days."

"I cannot see his reasons at all for having to go to town so suddenly after the ball, and then to leave us here for so many days in such a barbaric place. Those Bennets! I am certain they have designs on Charles."

Darcy attempted to not roll his eyes. They were twenty miles from London and yet her desires to become mistress of Pemberley—above one hundred miles away—were well-known. If Meryton was barbaric, Derbyshire must be as uncharted as the jungles of Africa. As for Mrs. Bennet's designs on Bingley, they were little different than those of most mothers of single daughters.

"I really see no need for him to return at all. Why do we not all go and meet him? His business is taking so long; he must be uncomfortable in a hotel," Mrs. Hurst offered.

Miss Bingley sounded unconvinced. "Mr. Darcy, what are your thoughts?"

"I can have no thoughts on the subject. I am here as Bingley's guest, and he assures me he will soon return. I always planned to leave in a fortnight in any event."

Miss Bingley frowned. "But surely you must know the nature of his business more than we do. We expected him back days ago, and now he says it will take several more. How can he be certain it will finish then?"

"I assure you, in matters of business one likes to finish as quickly as possible."

She let out a frustrated sigh and then glanced around the room, clearly seeing there were worse things than serving as mistress of a country estate for the winter with the hopes of impressing a wealthy gentleman.

He spoke no more. The subject turned to other matters before the ladies and Hurst departed entirely. Darcy looked to his letter again. He believed it unnecessary to share his observations that it was not business which caused the delays. His friend was a lively, amiable young man incapable of declining any offer out of fear of giving offence. Bingley raved about meeting Miss Agatha Markham again at one ball and being introduced to Miss Julia Cadogan at a recent dinner. Darcy could only speculate if Bingley would truly return to Netherfield this winter.

He sighed and thought over the day to come. His concerns went beyond Bingley's continued delays. Absent from the neighbourhood, Bingley could not make calls after the ball he hosted. The rest of the party could no longer put off the civility. That Darcy did not relish Hertfordshire society was no secret. Paying calls on people he barely knew was even less appealing. Yet, he both anticipated and dreaded seeing Elizabeth again.

Miss Bingley and Mrs. Hurst arranged it so they would call on Longbourn last. Darcy could almost feel sorry for the Bennets and the sour mood their guests would arrive in. Well, the others were sour. Darcy had reasons beyond civility to be present and preferred to dwell on the motivations which made his heart-rate increase instead of his blood boil.

They were shown into the drawing room. A quick look around proved Elizabeth absent, and he expected to feel relief but did not. An irrational fear that her cousin spirited her away—or worse, Wickham was somehow speaking privately with her, invaded his attempts at calm.

Mrs. Bennet asked after Bingley, and his sisters chose not to answer in deference to Darcy's information.

"I received another note from him in this morning's post. He apologizes again for the length of time his business is taking him but hopes to return next week."

Mrs. Bennet anxiously replied, "I cannot see what all this going back and forth is about."

Darcy chafed at her attitude. Who was she to make a claim on Bingley's habits?

"My friend is at such a point in his life when he is making new acquaintances with ease and has much to amuse him no matter where he is." This did not please Mrs. Bennet and to prevent any wailing on her side he added, "But he is a loyal companion and never forgets the friends he has made."

Mrs. Bennet gave a knowing look to her eldest daughter, and Darcy wanted to groan. Did he just offer encouragement on his friend's behalf? All this dancing on society's rules for courting exhausted him. Why could women not show their interest and the man need only ask the question and be done with the whole thing? One particular lady who frequently expressed her opinions came to mind, but he pushed the thought aside.

"I would think it better for the neighbourhood if he were well-settled in it."

Darcy almost laughed at the comment. If she thought she could lead Bingley down an aisle to her daughter, he welcomed her to try.

An unexpected voice spoke from the doorway. "Mamma, Mr. Bingley may come and go as he like. He may not mean to settle here for long."

Darcy stood and bowed at Elizabeth's entrance

Mrs. Bennet huffed at her daughter's chastisement. "Where have you been?"

Elizabeth set a vase of roses on the table. "I gathered flowers for Jane."

"Why should you gather flowers for Jane? I am certain she knows nothing of the sort of disappointment you have caused me!" She dabbed her nose with a handkerchief. "You know those sorts always irritate me. You can do nothing but vex me."

Elizabeth silently moved the flowers to a different table and sent a look to her eldest sister. Both ladies blushed at their mother's behaviour. Still noting the parson's absence and Mrs. Bennet's displeasure with Elizabeth, he wondered if she had rejected her cousin's marriage proposal. Darcy desired to alleviate Elizabeth's embarrassment and return to the earlier conversation. "I should not be surprised if he would give Netherfield up as soon as any eligible purchase offers."

Mrs. Bennet inhaled sharply, but Mrs. Hurst and Miss Bingley stood in unison announcing the end of the visit.

"Thank you for receiving us, madam. It was a pleasure to meet with you again," Miss Bingley said with cold civility while Mrs. Hurst gave a small curtsey.

"Oh, certainly. Jane will see you out."

Jane began to stand, but Elizabeth intervened.

"You know Jane has been feeling poorly, let us not fatigue her. I will see them to the carriage."

Once in the hallway, Elizabeth walked next to Darcy as the others briskly exited.

"We were all sorry to hear of Mr. Bingley's continued absence."

"What is one neighbour missing when you have met so many new companions recently?" He could not resist the reference. "Or has some of your acquaintance recently proved unsatisfactory?"

She gave him a direct look. "You might say so, but then others are exceedingly delightful."

"I would caution you again about happy manners."

"I am surprised you feel yourself capable of speaking on the subject."

Whispering harshly he replied. "I cannot know what Mr. Wickham has explicitly accused me of to incite your hatred, but I would recommend you carefully consider what proof may be attainable. Perhaps there is a resource at your disposal to understand more of Mr. Wickham's grievances and the possibility of any legitimacy of them."

She did not immediately reply, and he nodded his head before placing his hat and walking to the carriage. He vowed that to be the last time he was made a fool by Elizabeth Bennet.

December 12, 1811

"He loves you, Jane!" Elizabeth cried as she forced another stem into the vase in frustration. She huffed a stray piece of hair from her face and took a deep breath. "Do not give up."

"Miss Bingley has made it quite clear how much she missed town and that she means to stay there for the whole of the winter. She has praised Miss Darcy ceaselessly. I rather think she would prefer Miss Darcy as a sister," Jane said as she handed Elizabeth another flower for another arrangement.

"Surely she wishes for one marriage to bring on another, but anyone who has seen you two together must know how much you love each other."

Jane glanced away and did not speak at first. Eventually she said, "Caroline hints that Mr. Bingley is very fond of Miss Darcy. We must be mistaken on his regard for me."

"You cannot think simply because Miss Bingley tells you her brother is in love with Miss Darcy that he is any less sensible to your merits than he was when he last saw you."

"It has been over a fortnight. A very many great things may happen in a fortnight."

She twisted her apron between her hands and Elizabeth's heart went out to her. Surely Jane was quite in love with Mr.

Bingley in under a fortnight. She must have feared in an equal span of time Mr. Bingley's love could be cast aside but Elizabeth had more hope. "In a fortnight our aunt and uncle from London will be here and you can return with them as you always do. If Mr. Bingley is to remain in London, you may go to him."

Jane gasped in horror. "I could not!"

"Not to him, of course! You would keep your acquaintance with his sisters. As Mamma would say, "That will put you in his path!" Surely in London his sisters may be too distracted with other cares to meddle in his affairs."

"What sister could think she would have such an authority? We think very differently about Miss Bingley."

Elizabeth sighed. "Jane, dear, you think far too highly of everyone, but I will allow you to think of her in the best light." She frowned for a moment and then carefully rearranged several flowers. "There, now do you think that will please Mamma?"

"Quite," Jane said as she began to untie her apron.

Elizabeth grasped her hands. "I have every hope you and Bingley will find happiness together. How can two who love each other so much and with no possible sensible objections over the match be held apart? If it is as you say, and there is no scheming afoot, then all will soon conclude to make you the happiest of women."

Jane blushed but would say nothing else. Elizabeth frowned as she rushed through her toilette for the dinner party. Jane was her dearest sister and closest confidante. She could easily understand what Jane would not say. Her sister was hopelessly in love with Mr. Bingley and quite terrified even to speak of it. The thought did not sit well with Elizabeth. Jane usually truly felt more conviction behind her thoughts. She could be quite firm when she believed herself correct, and yet she did not hold steadfastly to the matter of Bingley's regard.

Elizabeth sighed as she came down the stairs to the drawing room. The Netherfield party were to leave for London the following day. Mr. Bingley had not returned. His sisters desired to see him, and Mr. Darcy had business of his own in London, as well as a sister whom he missed. He could not stay on and without him, Miss Bingley and Mrs. Hurst undoubtedly found Hertfordshire intolerable. Any sensible person saw the unlikelihood of Bingley's return.

Worse than that, the intimacy between Miss Bingley and Jane clearly declined after the ball a fortnight ago. They had met with the Netherfield party in company only twice since. The Bennets returned their call, and now Mrs. Bennet hosted a dinner for them this afternoon, although clearly they accepted out of forced civility.

Elizabeth anticipated little pleasure from the function. Seeing Jane's depressed spirits, Elizabeth knew not whether to hope for continued coldness from Miss Bingley or for the lady to be roused to renew a friendship with Jane. She might see

Bingley through his sisters, but Jane deserved more than false friendships.

Darcy was another source of displeasure for Elizabeth. He never gave up his habit of attending to her conversations but would no longer converse directly with her. He seemed haughtier than ever, as now he spoke to no one. He replied in clipped tones when spoken to, but rarely participated in discussion. Why he remained in Hertfordshire so long when he clearly hated the society, Elizabeth could not fathom.

Mrs. Bennet planned a large dinner party including other prominent area residents such as Sir William and Lady Lucas, the Gouldings, Mrs. Long, the Phillipses, and several of the officers. Elizabeth intended to observe Darcy meet with Wickham again.

Her mother scolded her for not arriving downstairs earlier, but then determined Elizabeth needed the additional time to look presentable. Elizabeth attempted to bear her mother's anxieties as best she could until the visitors arrived. The Netherfield party arrived late. At a quarter past the hour, Elizabeth extinguished hope of Mr. Wickham's presence. She could hardly help glaring at Darcy.

At last, seated at the table, Mrs. Bennet bemoaned the absence of Bingley, and of her dear friends at Netherfield going away. She rudely congratulated Miss Lucas on her betrothal to Mr. Collins. Between laughing and flirting with several officers, Lydia declared her disappointment at Wickham's absence. Frustrated at Darcy's presence by her side, Elizabeth could not help provoking him as he glanced at her.

"It seems we frequently have your company instead your more amiable friends, Mr. Darcy."

"I regret that Bingley has been unable to return to Netherfield, but perhaps we might all meet again."

His words implied a desire for continued acquaintance, but he looked angrier than ever. Why bother to speak with her at all!

"I understand your relations live in London, and you frequently visit."

Elizabeth nodded her head, perfectly understanding his reasoning. His earlier words were merely pretence to remind her of his superiority. She would not allow it. "I would not say I frequently visit them in London. Jane frequently goes for the Season, but I prefer to travel with them in the summer months."

He raised his eyebrows, undoubtedly surprised by her information. She took pleasure in showing that, regardless of what he may expect the Gardiners to be like, having known Mrs. Bennet and Mrs. Phillips, they were quite prosperous and earned nearly as much as Mr. Bingley.

"Where have you been with them?"

"We summered at Eastbourne. I also went to Bath twice and, last I heard, for next summer they hope to visit either

Cornwall or the Lakes." Pleased to show the haughty man her family could circulate with those of fashion, she smiled.

"How did you find Bath?"

He meant to despise her taste again, but she did not care. "I did not like it much at all, but as we did not go during the height of the Season, I suppose you will say it is my own fault."

He must have sensed her animosity because he turned the conversation. "Your sister frequently stays for the winter?"

"The Gardiners usually visit for Christmas and return with Jane. She typically stays until after Easter."

"Then she is missing the height of the Season."

"Jane does not care for balls and soirees. Indeed, my aunt and uncle seldom go to those functions. She enjoys town's other amusements such as the theatre."

"Perhaps I will be fortunate enough to see her if she comes again this year."

"Jane would call on Miss Bingley, of course. Are you much in their company?"

"Bingley and I frequently meet at our club."

Uncertain how she felt, she did not reply, and Darcy took advantage of her silence.

"It sounds like your London uncle does quite well." He nodded to Mr. Phillips. "Your other uncle seems talented in his profession."

Elizabeth looked at Darcy sceptically. "I believe Mr. Bingley arranged his lease through my uncle."

"He did, and I know Mr. Phillips was very knowledgeable."

Elizabeth scarcely believed she heard a compliment from Darcy towards her relatives.

"I found my solicitor invaluable when I was dealing with my father's will."

Elizabeth turned red in anger but quelled it. It seemed that Darcy admitted to—nay, boasted about—cheating Wickham of the living designed for him!

He seemed to not see her first reaction as he stared at his plate.

"One can learn much from talking to solicitors."

It was absolutely necessary to speak now. "I imagine you took the time to learn many details."

"I did, and I think you might learn a lot on how wills are processed as well."

She could say no more before her mother stood, and the ladies separated. She had no patience for the rest of the evening. When the gentlemen returned, she did not so much as look at Darcy. They did not stay on for supper, owing to their early departure the next day. Elizabeth only regretted that Jane's remaining hope of meeting Bingley again rested on seeing him in London.

January 7, 1812

"Miss Bingley and Mrs. Hurst," Darcy's London housekeeper announced and Darcy stifled his groan as he stood.

"Ladies, I regret your brother is not here. I believe he was making calls today."

Always sociable, lately Bingley threw himself into visiting and events with an unprecedented fervour.

Darcy felt the need for solitude more than ever but so far did not care to examine any cause for it.

"Oh, we came to see Georgiana! It was quite necessary for us to leave..." Miss Bingley shot her sister a look, and Mrs. Hurst immediately silenced.

"We only wanted to leave quickly as an impertinent acquaintance called."

Darcy scrutinised Miss Bingley's face. There were many people she might suddenly find as unlikeable—or rather of no use—but he only knew her to call Elizabeth impertinent. That seemed unlikely though, as Miss Bennet and not Elizabeth was to be in London, and their dispositions were quite different.

Glancing around the room his eyes fell to the bouquet of roses he suggested Georgiana display in the rooms he frequented. These were red, like the ones in Elizabeth's hair the night of the Netherfield Ball. Would he ever stop thinking of Elizabeth?

Georgiana soon entered and greeted her 'friends'. Darcy suppressed a sigh. He really felt he ought to do better by her than resorting to Miss Bingley and Mrs. Hurst as friends. If nothing else and there were certainly a number of something elses, they were quite a bit older than her. Yet, how could he encourage friendships with younger ladies without even more women believing they could become the next Mrs. Darcy? If only she could find a genuine friend with no designs on him.

The ladies chatted for some time before a name caught his attention.

"Did you receive another note from Miss Bennet?" Georgiana asked.

"My dear Georgiana, I cannot understand why you would even care!" Mrs. Hurst declared.

"Brother wrote that she was quite genteel, and Mr. Bingley mentioned her with fondness. But she has been in town for a week now and has not called on you?"

Miss Bingley hastily explained, "No, she has not and I declare it grieves my heart to think of all the kindness I bestowed on her and am now neglected."

Darcy raised his brow. So Jane Bennet did come to London, and after arriving found better things to do than call on Bingley's sisters. It did not quite surprise. Mrs. Bennet certainly hoped for a match between her eldest daughter and Bingley, but he never saw anything on the lady's side to be taken as encouragement, and now she seemed willing to give up the acquaintance entirely.

He noticed the relief on Mrs. Hurst and Miss Bingley's faces when the conversation turned. It was clear they did not want to discuss the Bennets in front of him. Likely both were too aware of his recent fascination with Elizabeth. He was beginning to think of their acquaintance with some regret. One regret was that he had been so transparent in his preference for her, and it had raised Miss Bingley's jealousy more than once.

In due time the visitors left, and Georgiana returned to her lessons. Bingley paid a late call, after dinner, and the two gentlemen sat in the library.

"Bingley, you will exhaust yourself with all this constant going and coming. Whom did you visit today?"

"My old friend from university, Palmer."

"And does Palmer have a pretty sister?"

"Aye! How did you know?"

"Every time I meet with you I am given a new account of three or four of the prettiest ladies you have ever seen in your life."

"I am not as bad as that!"

"You have always been a bit flighty with the ladies, but now one can barely keep your interest for an entire dinner party. You must be careful to not gain a reputation."

"I am no rake!"

"No, but you could easily be taken for one as you do nothing but flatter every lady in the room. Or worse, you could genuinely feel attached to a lady and be refused because she doubts your constancy."

Bingley did not speak, and Darcy felt the need to press on. He had saved him explicitly from mercenary women before but Bingley never acted thusly.

"Is there a cause for your recent exuberance for society?"

"I know not what I am about. I am tied up in knots by a lady. But that is precisely the type of thing on which you would know nothing."

Oh, but he did. Not for the first time he wondered if Elizabeth had taken his hints to consult her uncle about wills being ignored. He suspected Wickham told her some variation of Darcy ignoring his father's will and denying Wickham either money or the valuable living set aside for him. He chose not to answer his friend directly, nor could he speculate who worried his friend. He would wait until Bingley named a lady, like always.

"Come, I daresay she will be forgot easily enough. Especially at the rate you are going, meeting a dozen new ladies a night!"

February 8, 1812

Elizabeth read Jane's latest letter in anger. Unsurprised by Miss Bingley dropping the acquaintance entirely, their callous treatment of Jane still disgusted her.

Poor Jane! Even she suspected duplicity at this point, but Elizabeth felt less assured than before. As much as she hated to admit it, she found it quite possible Mr. Bingley simply no longer favoured her sister. Of course, that his sisters and friend wished him to marry Miss Darcy there could be no doubt.

She looked out her bedroom window and sighed. The fall had seemed so encouraging and bright. What could be finer than new acquaintances and possible suitors at that time! Instead, Mr. Bingley proved inconstant, Mr. Darcy proved hateful, the ladies proved superior and scheming, and even the militia held little interest to her now.

Wickham's attentions were over, and she did not feel the loss. Besides having no strong regard on her side, his income was insufficient—due to Darcy. It was prudent that Wickham now attached himself to a lady who recently inherited ten thousand pounds.

Visiting her friend Charlotte brought some anticipation, but Elizabeth expected little pleasure, knowing her company included Mr. Collins, Lady Catherine de Bourgh, Sir William and Maria Lucas. Most of the party were known to her, and she had every expectation that Lady Catherine's condescension would be amusing but soon prove tiresome. Perhaps by having such low hopes the visit would prove more bearable. At least she would be able to see Jane and know for herself that she was not ill over Bingley's abandonment. She hoped the Gardiners had decided on the details of their summer tour. Tiring of the seaside and perfectly ordered resorts, she longed to see the wildness of the North.

She felt tempted to rearrange the dried flower arrangement before her for the tenth time that day, but did not touch it for fear it would crumble. She missed the sunshine and warmer weather of the past summer and the autumn. Spring seemed interminably far away. She missed her sister's calming words and her friend's good sense. For a lingering moment, she thought of how lonely she was with Charlotte married and away and Jane in London for months. But then, Jane never approved of her moods and distrust of others. Charlotte she apparently never understood at all if she could marry Mr. Collins only for such mercenary motives. The sobering truth descended on her. Only the quality of company, not the quantity, would abate the feelings of loneliness.

While many wise people might conclude there must be an error in themselves to make them so deficient, Elizabeth's pride revolted at the idea. Jane was simply too trusting and Charlotte too practical, and that was all there was to it. Elizabeth remained implacable in her opinion of her own discernment and judgment.

Chapter 2

March 19, 1812

February passed into March without incident and, in due time, Elizabeth arrived at Hunsford. She had seen Jane only for a day, but she seemed well. Her heart might still be broken over Bingley, but her health was not in danger. Having that fear relieved, she was surprised to admit how much she anticipated Kent. She knew Mr. Collins would try her nerves, but to be in the company of Charlotte again would be most agreeable. If nothing else, Rosings would offer a change of scenery.

Two weeks in the frequent company of Lady Catherine passed predictably, all Elizabeth's fears of little enjoyment having been met, and then interesting news was reported at one dinner. Anything Lady Catherine could say about new visitors would be a welcome relief.

"Mrs. Collins, it is most fortunate your visitors are here at this time of year. They will have quite the pleasure, I am sure, to meet my nephews, Mr. Darcy of Pemberley and Colonel

Fitzwilliam, younger son of my brother, the Earl. They will be arriving in a few days' time. Anne especially looks forward to their visit each year."

Mr. Collins interjected. "It will be a pleasure to meet Mr. Darcy again!"

"Meet him again! What do you mean again?"

"I had the privilege to meet him in Hertfordshire, ma'am, while I was staying with my cousins and before I had proposed to my fair Mrs. Collins."

"You mean to say you have all met Darcy!"

Charlotte looked distressed at Lady Catherine's displeasure, so Elizabeth intervened. "I am sorry, it is true, your ladyship. He stayed many weeks with his friend who was leasing an estate in the area."

Lady Catherine narrowed her eyes at Elizabeth. She could only think the great lady disapproved to hear Mr. Darcy's friends were not all landed estate owners.

"I am sure it will be a privilege to meet Colonel Fitzwilliam," Elizabeth attempted to smooth the situation.

"Yes, I daresay it will," was all her ladyship would say in reply.

In truth, Elizabeth did think she might enjoy observing how Darcy would meet with his cousin, whom Lady Catherine clearly destined him for.

Darcy and Colonel Fitzwilliam duly arrived in a further three days and on the following day Mr. Collins rushed back to announce that they were about to call, unexpectedly, at the Parsonage.

"I must thank you for this civility, Eliza. Mr. Darcy would never call so quickly on me," Charlotte teased her friend.

Elizabeth attempted to correct her, but soon the gentlemen were announced. Darcy barely said a word, but his cousin was very amiable. At length, Darcy managed to ask after the health of Elizabeth's family. Given this opening, she could not resist discovering if he would betray any knowledge of how the Bingleys had treated Jane.

"My eldest sister has been in town these three months. Have you never happened to see her there?"

She was surprised when he answered in a tone of slight reproach. "No, I never had the pleasure of seeing Miss Bennet." He paused for a moment and added, "I had expected to meet with her after our last conversation at Longbourn, but I did not."

Elizabeth was confused by his tone and evident annoyance. He spoke no more during the visit, and she was glad for it. Nor did she repine not seeing him for another week, although his cousin did call on the Parsonage more than once during the time.

March 30, 1812

Darcy could hardly believe it. He resisted seeing Elizabeth Bennet all week, yet less than ten minutes in her company and all his vaunted self-control was gone. More than once he felt a nearly irresistible draw to the Parsonage, but he managed to remain master of himself. Something about her presence bewitched him. The danger he felt in Hertfordshire was intensified after knowing how impossible she was to give up.

She was always beautiful, too beautiful for his own peace of mind—her eyes so expressive they revealed the clever working of an active mind—but this evening she was certainly enjoying herself as his cousin flirted with her. Would that it were he, enjoying her smiles! But no, he had learned to suppress anything charming in him long ago.

Lady Catherine interrupted his thoughts. "How does Georgiana get on, Darcy?"

Tearing his eyes away from Elizabeth, he replied to his aunt. "Her music teacher is very pleased with her."

"She cannot expect to excel without practicing a good deal."

"I assure you, madam, she does not need the advice. She practices very constantly."

In fact, it was the only thing that could bring her any amount of peace from her thoughts.

"I have told Miss Bennet she should practice more and, though Mrs. Collins has no instrument, she is very welcome to Rosings each day and practice in Mrs. Jenkinson's room."

He could hardly contain his anger at his aunt's ill-breeding! When they were married, he would be sure Elizabeth was always afforded due respect.

Darcy's breath caught, and he looked away to hide his discomposure. He was only vaguely aware that the others continued speaking, fortunately without any need for input from him. He was surprised at the vehemence of his resolve a moment ago. He had thought about it before, longed for it, and considered it to be impossible, but at this moment he knew Elizabeth was like a rare wildflower. If he let her go, he may never see the like again.

He knew, too, what he felt for her was not any trifling inclination. To his own mortification, in his youth—when not even of age—he had considered matrimony to a young lady of Society. A visit to a friend's estate and meeting his attractive sister was nearly his undoing. Her apparent admiration had earned his gratitude, and he had planned to propose after only one month's acquaintance. She was charming, to be sure, but he saw soon afterwards that she had designed to entrap him while he was so conveniently situated. On the very eve of his meditated proposal, he lost his nerve and left as planned.

He intended to visit again only a few weeks later, to truly state his addresses but found, within a fortnight away from Miss Stanton's company, that he was no longer bewitched. There were other pretty ladies, others just as charming. Before he could put off his planned return, news of her engagement to the son of a wealthy baronet reached his ears. Their acquaintance was of only three weeks. Since then he had never allowed himself to admit to preferring a lady. He knew the fickleness of infatuation and distrusted the constancy of a woman's admiration.

Yet, all this logic escaped him entirely with Elizabeth. He was older, wiser and master of himself and a great estate. He was trusted with the care of hundreds of lives. He wanted Elizabeth for his wife as he had never wanted another. What should stop him but his own contempt for her family? Surely his love for her was enough.

Coffee was over, and Colonel Fitzwilliam pulled himself closely to Elizabeth's side at the pianoforte. Darcy was surprised his cousin did not ignite under the disapproving glares he sent. Under the guise of querying Elizabeth on some musical matter—for Georgiana's sake—he was able to break free from his aunt and approach Elizabeth. Her teasing banter was intoxicating; she was finer than the finest wine he had ever drunk, and to know that soon he could have his fill for a lifetime made him happy enough that he did not even mind his cousin's continued flirting.

She was teasing him again, never mind she addressed the Colonel. "He danced only four dances though gentlemen were scarce; and, to my certain knowledge, more than one young lady was sitting down in want of a partner. Mr. Darcy, you cannot deny the fact."

"I had not at that time the honour of knowing any lady in the assembly beyond my own party." He found it hard to understand, now, why she had been sitting out in the first place. She outshone every woman in the county, every woman he had ever met.

"Shall we ask your cousin the reason of this?" said Elizabeth, still addressing Colonel Fitzwilliam. "Shall we ask him why a man of sense and education, and who has lived in the world, is ill-qualified to recommend himself to strangers?"

"I can answer your question," said Fitzwilliam, "without applying to him. It is because he will not give himself the trouble."

She was asking about his character again. He would satisfy her this time, allow her to know the true him. "I certainly have not the talent which some people possess," said Darcy, "of conversing easily with those I have never seen before. I cannot catch their tone of conversation, or appear interested in their concerns, as I often see done."

"My fingers," she replied, "do not move over this instrument in the masterly manner which I see so many women's do. They have not the same force or rapidity, and do not produce the same expression. But then I have always supposed it to be my own fault—because I will not take the trouble of practising. It is not that I do not believe my fingers as capable as any other woman's of superior execution."

Darcy smiled and said, "You are perfectly right. You have employed your time much better. No one admitted to the privilege of hearing you can think anything wanting. We neither of us perform to strangers."

This was what he had been waiting for his whole life. Not just a pretty face from a family of good standing, desirous of his money and connections. Instead, he sought a woman who understood and accepted him. The fact that she once preferred his enemy made her welcoming his attention all the sweeter. He was pleased he had taken the risk to hint at Wickham's misdeeds.

Her acceptance set him at such peace that Darcy was able to forbear his aunt's vaguely insulting words to Elizabeth and praise of his cousin's imaginary talents. His aunt was easily ignored and soon left their sides for the fawning of Mr. Collins. Elizabeth agreed to play the rest of the evening, and Darcy was able to plan his courtship.

The next morning as Elizabeth worked on a handkerchief with cheerful spring flowers for Jane, Mr. Darcy called on the Parsonage, greatly surprising her. He quickly apologised for finding her alone; he had expected all the ladies to be home. Inwardly she rolled her eyes. Of course, he would hate to be in her sole company. The last time such an event occurred he ignored her entirely for half an hour.

They were very much in danger of sinking into a similar episode when she decided to indulge her curiosity. She mentioned how quickly they all left Netherfield the previous November.

"Mr. Bingley and his sisters were well when you left London?"

"Perfectly so, I thank you."

Annoyed with his brief reply she coldly inquired, "I have heard he does not mean to return to Netherfield anymore."

"He has many friends and is at an age when friends and engagements are continually increasing. He may spend little time there in the future."

Elizabeth's head jerked up from staring at her hands. "I had thought you meant if another person offered to purchase Netherfield, he would give it up. Not that he was looking elsewhere."

Darcy made a vague reply, and she soon gave up the topic and determined to allow him to choose a subject.

"This seems a comfortable house," he said.

"Yes, I understand your aunt did a great deal to it, and Mr. Collins could not have been more grateful, I am sure."

"Mr. Collins seems very fortunate in his choice of wife."

"Yes...I admit to wondering at my friend's sensibleness in accepting him, but she has an excellent understanding and seems perfectly happy. Most would say it is a good match for her."

He raised an eyebrow at her statement, and she hoped to conceal her blush. She had given away too much of her own thoughts on that matter.

"It must be agreeable to her; Meryton is only half a day's journey from here."

"You think it an easy distance?"

"Fifty miles of good road is a very easy distance."

Insufferable arrogance, she thought. "No one would say Mrs. Collins is settled near her family."

"You are so attached to Hertfordshire anything beyond Longbourn must appear far."

He smiled, but she understood he referenced Jane at Netherfield. She could not help blushing with her reply. "A woman can be settled too near her family. It is all relative. If there is fortune, distance becomes no evil but that is not the case here. They cannot afford frequent journeys, and I am certain my friend would not consider herself near her family under less than half the distance."

It surprised her when he drew his chair closer to her and made some claim that, due to her travels with her aunt and uncle, she could have no local attachment. He must have registered her confused look because he drew back and glanced over a newspaper.

All the previous animation was gone when he asked her if she enjoyed Kent, and they spoke on the county for a few minutes before Charlotte and Miss Lucas returned. Darcy sat silently for an only a moment or two longer before quickly departing.

"My dear Eliza! Mr. Darcy must be in love with you to call on us in such a way."

Elizabeth laughed out right. "He was silent for most of the time, Charlotte. And then mocking to me and Hertfordshire society."

She could see she had not convinced her friend of a thing, but then she pressed the point of how bored he must be at Rosings. He and his cousin continued to call frequently on Hunsford, and more than once during Darcy's stay in the area did Charlotte vex Elizabeth by declaring Darcy was partial to her. Elizabeth hardly supposed Darcy capable of feeling affection for anyone, especially her. It had much better be his cousin, but Elizabeth had no expectations from him. He was pleasant company, but no more and, as a second son, would need to make an advantageous marriage. He was at least amiable whereas Darcy was as arrogant as ever.

The day after Darcy's call on the Parsonage, Elizabeth had the misfortune to come across him on her morning walk. She expected him to merely nod to her but instead he turned to walk with her.

"Good day, Miss Elizabeth," he said with a bow.

"Good day, Mr. Darcy." Elizabeth examined his countenance. He appeared more cheerful than she had seen him before.

"You are here quite early," she observed.

"As are you."

She had been up late after reading a letter from Jane. "I could not sleep." She thought she heard him mumble about a similar affliction for months.

The man certainly was strange. His face in Hertfordshire had always been stony and disapproving when he looked at her, or anyone else. Now she saw other expressions but had no reliance at all on the accuracy of her impressions.

In Hertfordshire, he had barely spoken, and yet lately he seemed eager enough for her company at times in Kent. Now he mumbled things under his breath as though they bubbled up without his consent. That was a shocking thought. Mr. Darcy had always seemed resolutely, although stiffly, in control of himself before.

Breaking the silence she inquired after his cousin. "Is the Colonel still asleep? Quite enjoying his holiday, I would say! I did not think men of uniform were also men of leisure."

Darcy chuckled. "He has told stories of going days without rest during battle. When he is allowed, he would sleep all day."

"He certainly has earned it."

"Yes. I would wish he did not have to face such perils." Elizabeth was gratified to see true affection and admiration in Darcy's eyes as he spoke of his cousin.

"When we were young we would often play pretend battles. I am afraid the real thing is nothing like the fantasies of our youth."

He paused then added, "He joined up right after the Treaty of Amiens, when it seemed the Revolution in France was over. His father asked him to reconsider. Due to his activity in the House of Lords he believed that more war was inevitable, but Richard did not want the life of a barrister or vicar. He has been to the Continent twice but is based in

London now. However, now there is talk of trouble with the Americans." Darcy shook his head for a moment. "At least we were fortunate he did not join the Navy."

"I wonder he does not marry. I know nothing of the Earl's finances, but I can only assume it all must go to the heir. You may know my father's estate is entailed away from the female line. I have been so accustomed to considering the poor lot women face that I have not concerned myself with the disadvantages of being a younger son, even of an earl. Surely some lady with a large dowry would desire a match with him. He is well-connected and amiable."

"That would be one solution and I am unsurprised you would think most men of his station and rank would not hesitate to do so. But our fathers were unusual and encouraged their children to seek love and mutual respect over more mercenary advantages, as they themselves did."

"It must be a very easy thing to just happen to fall in love with an earl's daughter or a very wealthy gentleman." Elizabeth blushed as she realised she criticised his parents. "I am sorry, Mr. Darcy..."

He waved her apology off. "You never saw them together, so it likely sounds to others just as you have portrayed it. But all their closest friends and family knew them to be deeply in love. True, the match was not a bad one, although my grandfather wanted better for my mother. But it is not their fault they inherited their wealth and happened to fall in love with one of equal significance. The heart wants what it wants, regardless of rank and wealth."

She raised her brows in surprise. "I had not taken you for such a romantic, Mr. Darcy. Such poetic words!"

He chuckled again. "Pray, spare me your opinion of poetry again!"

They shared a little laugh, although she was surprised he recalled her words spoken in an attempt to quiet her mother months ago. She supposed it was simply because they were so contrary to all reason, and he always seemed fascinated by her backwards ways. Such a fault he could not forget. Turning to look at him again she saw that gaze so reminiscent from Hertfordshire upon her again.

Why had I ever thought he might think better of me? She tried to hide her surprise at her own thoughts. When had his approval ever mattered to her?

She cleared her throat. "It seemed as though you believed the Colonel had more than one solution to his problems?"

He was silent for a moment before speaking. "He does have a sizable allowance from my uncle. He could try to live within it, although it would not support a wife and children in the sort of circumstances he would like. Others have offered to supplement it for him, or the use of a small estate, but he refuses anything that looks like charity. He has his pride, as do we all.

"Greater than all this, he truly feels it his duty to fight until the war is won. As I am intimately acquainted with the demands of duty, I cannot rebuke him for it, even if it seems nonsensical to me."

"Surely there comes a time when duty must be forsaken if it comes at extreme peril to oneself!" Elizabeth cried.

"That might be a decision easier said than done, Miss Bennet. Surely, you have not had to make such a decision between your life and duty to King and country."

"No, but that is not to say that, as a woman, I do not feel the demands of duty any less."

Darcy cocked his head and looked at her for a moment. "Ah, yes. The demands of marriage. Tell me, was he very heartbroken?"

Elizabeth gasped. How could he know she rejected Mr. Collins' proposal? "I am sure I do not know what you mean, sir." It would be a horrible break in propriety to speak it.

"I am sure I do not know either," he said with a sly smile. "I can only surmise that you refused some poor man desperately in love with you because you had a family obligation to marry better." Elizabeth would be offended if it were not for the slight twinkle in his eyes which proved his jest.

Laughingly she replied, "Oh, you would be quite wrong. And now I am disappointed in you, sir. I had thought you intelligent enough to have sketched my character by now. I would never forsake ardent love for my family. To marry where there is no affection, or worse, when your heart belongs to another, seems nearly as perilous to oneself as a battlefield. While family is important, there are limits to what is reasonable for them to ask, and one must live one's own life."

Elizabeth had been watching the path and, when Darcy did not reply, she looked up at him. He had the strangest expression in his eyes. His continued silence unnerved her, and she quickly looked away.

Certain as she was he would wish to avoid her in the future, as their conversations either sank into silence or they argued, she explained: "This is my favourite path." She hoped he would understand to leave her in peace. She enjoyed the natural flora compared to the well-ordered park.

"Indeed? It is a lovely one."

Elizabeth had nothing more to say and refused to further the conversation. Darcy seemed similarly inclined and, when they reached the Parsonage gate, she had every confidence her solitary walks were assured in future.

However, a few days later she met with him again. She asked after the health of all those at Rosings and remarked on the weather, and once more they descended into silence. Darcy was looking at her a great deal.

"Is there something amiss in my apparel or my bonnet, Mr. Darcy?"

He startled. "No, why should you think it?"

"You have stared at me for nearly our entire walk."

"You simply...fascinate me."

"Yes, I often noticed your fascinated gaze on me. I suppose my impertinence is something to behold. I am certain none of your London ladies behave as I do. Please, commit every flaw to memory so you can ensure your sister may learn to be better."

Darcy stared at her for a long moment. "I actually desired to introduce you to my sister when you returned to London in the hope of you two forming an acquaintance. She is very shy. She does not have many friends her age and there are doubts to the sincerity of affection from any of them. I believe a friendship with you could be of great benefit to her!"

Elizabeth's eyes widened in wonder. She had heard from Wickham that Georgiana Darcy was very proud and, knowing her brother, Elizabeth had no difficulty believing it to be so. But no matter their faults of character and manner she had never seen anything to make her think Darcy was not truly fond of and protective of his sister.

To ask Elizabeth to form an acquaintance with his sister, to infer that he did not trust the likes of Caroline Bingley and Louisa Hurst, was hard to credit.

"I...I would be honoured to meet Miss Darcy," Elizabeth stuttered out at last. Darcy looked infinitely pleased.

They talked of nothing of greater importance for several more minutes when Darcy checked his watch and declared he must return to Rosings.

As he left her side, Elizabeth wondered if he met with her for the sole purpose of vexing her.

By the third time she met Darcy on the path, she was prepared for there to be little conversation. Instead, Darcy chatted on.

"How did you like Rosings when you visited there last?"

"I confess the rooms confuse me. I was welcomed to use the library, and escorted there, but when I made to return to the drawing room before dinner I got turned around. I opened up the billiard room instead! I believe I quite startled Colonel Fitzwilliam! I suppose he was hiding in there from your aunt while you attended to her in the drawing room."

"It did seem you were gone for quite a while." He nearly looked anxious, but Elizabeth could not understand why.

She pursed her lips. "Are you always so eager to return to Lady Catherine's presence?"

He let out a little laugh. "No, indeed."

"Truthfully, I quite lost myself in a book." She shrugged her shoulders, knowing better than to admit to her preference for botany. "The Colonel was good enough to direct me to the appropriate room. I would not want to displease Lady Catherine, and it become a matter of contention between her and my hosts. I am sure she has different expectations for her relations, and hence why the Colonel's presence was not missed, than she does for her other guests."

"Were you able to finish it?"

"No, but I hope to find a copy of it in London." In truth, she had been saving her pin money for the bulky two volume set of *Flora Scotica* by the Reverend John Lightfoot.

"I am certain when you next visit the area you will find your way about easier. You will have greater familiarity with the rooms."

Elizabeth could not quite gather his meaning. Did he imply she might be staying at Rosings? He seemed anxious just now when she mentioned stumbling upon Colonel Fitzwilliam. Whenever the Colonel was present, he was quite attentive to her. Did Darcy believe his cousin would offer for her? She was flattered at the idea but had only known him a few weeks and could not say her feelings went beyond friendship for him. Surely, if he was raised desiring a love match, he would want the feeling reciprocated.

Darcy was speaking again. What on earth made him so talkative today? Was he asking her about the Collinses' marriage?

She was beginning to wonder after Darcy's intelligence. He had to realise by now they could not go a single conversation without dissolving into disagreement. Perhaps her opinions were a source of amusement for him. She could think of no reason for him to continue his torture.

"The marriage certainly is prudential for them both. I must suppose that makes them quite happy."

Elizabeth scoffed in disbelief. "While I have seen no evidence to the contrary what was all your talk the other day about love matches then if you think prudence alone can make happiness in marriage."

"I did not say prudence alone could, but some attention to fortune must be made."

Elizabeth nearly laughed when she recalled Mr. Collins's proposal to her, in which he declared himself entirely indifferent to fortune. "Must it? I would not suggest a couple marry if there is insufficient income but I have seen matches made with fortune greatly in mind, regardless of the character or disposition of the parties, and cannot claim they are happy, to my observance."

"Would you not find a person insensible to marry only on the basis of affection?"

"These are relative terms, as would be a wife's ability to travel and visit her family. Fifty miles to some is a very easy distance, but it is not so for everyone. Likewise, some may think they need thousands of pounds to raise a family on, to lavish their wives and children with expensive gifts and have the younger sons avoid a profession. But I would wager a family that economised in the face of a wife's poverty, but had true affection, could be truly happier than a family with money aplenty but only tolerable feelings for each other."

"I will concede the point, Miss Bennet."

Elizabeth beamed. She personally believed she always bested Darcy in their arguments but to hear such a proud man admit it was a triumph indeed!

"Do you allow then that Mrs. Collins's marriage to an established gentleman is a credit as well?"

"I suppose, although she might have been just as respectable if she married a man of good sense and honour from trade. The higher ranks alone do not hold a monopoly on those virtues."

"Hmm...So this gentleman whose heart you crushed was not dismissed due to being a tradesman."

Did Mr. Darcy just tease? "Well...I...first of all, sir, there is none whose heart I have broken."

"You have never refused a suit?"

Elizabeth blushed scarlet as she prevaricated. "That is not what I have said and that is all I shall say. But, I am a gentleman's daughter, and I think I would be more comfortable in the sphere in which I have been brought up. That is not to say I am mercenary, sir. For we know there are many impoverished peers. They would not only be above my station, and perhaps unwise to grasp at, but I would more easily be happy with a gentleman of little means but of similar education and temperament to myself than a wealthy tradesman or lofty viscount."

"So it is important to have a common understanding and similar interests with the gentleman to ensure happiness?"

"I think so. I have seen unbalanced marriages. I think myself intelligent but would I understand and be content with a husband whose mind must necessarily be turned to his business at all times? Would I grow to resent a less leisurely life?"

"I would think you would miss the capacity for your generosity."

"Pardon me?"

"As a mistress of an estate you would see to the welfare of your servants and tenants. You know that gentlemen must see to their affairs as well as a businessman although perhaps you grew up learning of agriculture."

Elizabeth nodded her head.

"I had thought so. A tradesman may have to worry over the profit he may divide between his investors, but it is not the same as the interest in a person's life that a landlord has. Your care and generosity for others cannot be missed. I would also think a tradesman's wife has more time for leisure than the proper mistress of a profitable estate, and I know your dislike for idleness."

Elizabeth was rather astonished. These last statements sounded shockingly like a compliment. Incapable of believing such from him, she twisted his meaning. "I think you have found the truth at last, sir! I would be far happier in the country where I may walk to my heart's content, than in London or a market town!"

He chuckled.

Elizabeth could not quite understand why it seemed as though he met her by design this morning. She finally settled upon the idea that he decided to take her advice and practice conversing with people.

As he proved pleasant today, she could not truly repent that he had singled her out for the exercise. She could think of no one else who would suffice besides Mrs. Collins. She only wondered how long he would continue the new habit. She truly was fond of solitary walks, especially when residing with Mr. Collins and in the frequent company of Lady Catherine.

They had turned back many minutes ago and now were at the Parsonage gate. "Will you come in, Mr. Darcy?" She suppressed her smile at the fear that entered his eyes.

"It is early for a call; I had better not. My cousin and I will call later."

He turned to leave, and Elizabeth rolled her eyes. It was as she thought. He could not be bothered to converse with the others and only sought her company out of boredom.

Chapter 3

A few days later Elizabeth read Jane's latest letter again, which proved she was not in the best of spirits, as she walked. Wishing she could bring Jane some of the flowers she so loved in an attempt to provide cheer, Colonel Fitzwilliam, and not his cousin, happened upon her.

During their conversation, after fearing she offended him with an ill-thought remark on Miss Darcy, she quickly interjected that she had only heard of the young lady through Miss Bingley and Mrs. Hurst.

"Their brother is a great friend of Darcy's."

"Yes, I understand Mr. Darcy takes prodigiously good care of Mr. Bingley."

"Care of him! Yes, I am sure Darcy does take care of him. I believe Bingley to be very much indebted to Darcy from something he mentioned during our journey. Although, I am not certain he meant Bingley."

"What do you mean?"

"Darcy only said that he congratulated himself on lately saving a friend from a most imprudent marriage. I only suppose it to be Bingley as he is the sort to get himself into that kind of scrape, and I know Darcy spent all of last summer with him."

She could hardly keep the hard edge from her voice as she asked, "What reasons did Mr. Darcy have for such interference?"

"I understand there were some very strong objections against the lady."

"Did he mention how he separated them?"

"He only told me what I have told you now."

Elizabeth was too angry to speak. She walked in silence until Colonel Fitzwilliam interrupted her rapid thoughts. "You are very thoughtful."

"Your cousin's conduct does not suit my feelings. Why was he to be the judge?"

"You think him officious?"

"Why was his judgment alone enough for him to direct his friend? How could he presume to know what would make his friend happy?" She was very near to crying for Jane's loss but attempted to collect herself. "I suppose there must not have been much affection."

"That would be logical, but it lessens Darcy's triumph."

She could so clearly see Darcy congratulating himself on such a feat that she could not speak on the subject any longer. She quickly turned the conversation to the weather for the Colonel's upcoming travels.

As soon as she could, she locked herself away in her room. She had always thought Darcy played a part in separating Bingley from Jane but believed it mostly Miss Bingley's design. Now it all lay at Darcy's door. He had wounded the most affectionate, generous heart in the world. She may never love again!

The Colonel said there were strong objections to the lady, but they could not possibly be toward Jane herself. She briefly considered her family's behaviour before determining Darcy would rather his friend have greater connections than worry over the sense of the bride's relations. With one uncle a country attorney and the other in business in London, it was clear why Darcy would disapprove of Bingley marrying Jane.

She gave in to her tears, not at all wondering why it suddenly hurt so much more to have this news confirmed: to hear that it was Mr. Darcy who organised Bingley's defection. She had never thought well of him, never believed him particularly honourable and never believed she or anyone of her acquaintance had his good opinion, or that it would be a blessing to have it. Her roiling emotions produced an intense headache and, after some argument, Charlotte persuaded Mr. Collins to allow Elizabeth to remain behind from their engagement at Rosings. She could only add a prayer that he and Colonel Fitzwilliam did not call on the house tomorrow before leaving. She wished to never see Mr. Darcy again.

Darcy paced around his aunt's drawing room. Elizabeth was not here! How could she not come? It was to be her last chance to see him! Perhaps he had not been obvious enough in his attentions in the last week. She must fear seeing him again and raising her hopes for his addresses.

He nearly proposed on their walk the other day; it was his intention to do so, but she seemed distracted. Surely she understood his hints? As much as he disliked the thought of it, he was now entirely resolved to follow her to Longbourn in a week's time and court her there.

Surely he could stay at Netherfield, and whatever expectations Mrs. Bennet had of Bingley must now be over. Her daughter's actions bespoke her indifference, and Bingley showed no symptoms of preferring Jane Bennet above every other lady that had captured his attention. He could easily return to the area without danger.

As amiable as his friend was, Bingley would not resent Darcy for marrying the lady's sister. He could almost feel sorry for Bingley, as another one of the ladies he admired proved indifferent. Last summer he nearly proposed to a purely mercenary woman. Darcy at least had the clear encouragement from Elizabeth. But Bingley was young yet. One day he would find a lady who enjoyed his attentions and not his pocketbook. Darcy knew from his own experience.

He made some excuse to leave the room and did not slow when he heard his aunt's annoyed remarks. Heading to the stables he asked the groom to saddle a horse. Poor Elizabeth! How could he leave her to think he was only trifling with her?

Darcy soon arrived at the Parsonage and was shown to the drawing room. He was startled by her appearance. She truly looked unwell. She had been crying; it was clear to see. He was angry at himself for allowing her to feel so neglected, but a selfish part of him rejoiced to see more evidence of her affection.

"Are you well? I heard you were unwell, that you were indisposed— that is you had a headache. I hope you are feeling better."

"I am."

Her voice was cold, and he understood the pain he must have caused her. He had to order his thoughts; they were too unruly. He sat looking at her, so lovely, but her face, etched in contempt and pain, did nothing to assuage him. He paced around the room. He had planned pretty words yet now nothing was in his head but that he loved her. For a moment his old fears and prejudices emerged. A woman was too fickle to love, or was it only that he could not inspire a lasting affection in a woman?

At last he stopped and looked at her. She would not meet his eye, and soon the words tumbled from his mouth.

"In vain have I struggled. It will not do. You must allow me to tell you how ardently I admire and love you."

His heart pounded, and his breathing was hard, but she blushed and did not beg for him to cease. Yes, yes she was expecting his proposal. She had been desiring, perhaps for weeks or even months for him to speak. He would tell her all.

"I have loved you from almost the beginning of our acquaintance. Your beauty and wit soon enthralled me. Then I was captivated by your intelligence, your civility and clear affection for those around you— even when it was undeserved. You, of course, may wonder why a man of my independence did not speak earlier but I thought it foolish to propose matrimony to a woman of lower birth, with such poor connections and a family so incapable of decorum. Society would laugh at me and think I was blinded by infatuation."

In one of the worst-case scenarios he played out in his head she would be rejected by the patronesses at Almack's, not because she had an uncle in trade, but because it was presumed he had made her his doxy first. Elizabeth was a gentleman's daughter but with such low connections and no fortune, in his hyperbolic thoughts he feared some would believe only one thing attracted him to her. But Lady

Catherine even treated her with a certain amount of respect, surely his fears were for naught. And they could face that together, if it came to it; if their love was enough. He was growing anxious again.

"I care not for the opinions of others now. I am my own master. I have—very sensibly I would say—tried to ignore my true feelings. It has been many months of battle, and I cannot win. I love you too deeply, and you must have seen my attentions. You have given me every hope. I must ask you to end my suffering and accept my hand in marriage."

He paused and assumed the confident air which always served him well when conducting business or even playing cards, regardless of his concerns. "And now I have only to await your answer."

Elizabeth turned red again, but her tone was not the soft or elated sounds of happiness he had so often imagined. Instead, he heard in calm civility:

"I know it is common for women to feel obliged to a proposal even when they do not return the sentiments and perhaps, if I could feel gratitude, I would even thank you. But I cannot—I have never desired your good opinion. I am sorry to pain you, it was most unconsciously done, but I am certain you will soon overcome the pain due to your other feelings."

His other feelings? What feelings had he had for months now but that he loved Elizabeth and only wanted the best for her? Even when he considered what was best for her was not marriage to him! Blood drained from his face when he realised she truly had refused him. In all his nightmares, this had never happened. He thought he prepared for every eventuality, but this one.

Nor was her mode of refusal lost on him. He had never heard her so uncivil before. Good God! Had he ever even known her at all? The thought of the one woman he had believed superior to all others treating him so poorly angered him. Had it all been a design? Attract his notice just to cruelly reject him?

He forced himself to sound calm when he would rather sob or scream. "And this is all the reply which I am to have the honour of expecting! I might, perhaps, wish to be informed why, with so little endeavour at civility, I am thus rejected. But it is of small importance."

"If I was uncivil I would have every excuse. You so clearly desired to offend and insult me by declaring you liked me against your will, against your reason and even against your character. You even declared my family improper! But I have other provocations. Nothing could tempt me to accept the man who has been the means of ruining, perhaps forever, the happiness of a most beloved sister."

He turned red, at first thinking she referenced his own sister but she continued to speak.

"No motive can excuse the unjust and ungenerous part you acted there. You cannot deny that you have been the principal, if not the only, means of dividing them. You exposed one to the censure of the world for caprice and the other to its derision for disappointed hopes. You have involved them both in misery of the acutest kind."

He had felt remorse when he thought she spoke of his own sister's pain, but he now understood she referenced her own sister and his friend! Bingley was certainly not censured for capriciousness nor was he miserable. Considering how Miss Bennet did not so much as call on Caroline Bingley he could hardly believe she was miserable either.

"Can you deny you have done it?"

"I have no wish of denying that I did everything in my power to separate my friend from your sister, or that I rejoice in my success. Towards him, I have been kinder than towards myself."

Of course, all he ever encouraged Bingley to do was exactly what he had done for himself: separate from the lady in question and think over the matter. Darcy did at least consider if Miss Bennet loved his friend. In his own case, he never thought to caution his heart against such an attachment. If his friend did feel pain, it could be nothing like Darcy was experiencing.

"It is not only this affair upon which my dislike is built. Your character was unfolded to me months ago by Mr. Wickham. In what imaginary act of friendship can you defend yourself?"

"You take an eager interest in that gentleman's concerns!" This was not happening. This could not be. He was rejected by Elizabeth in favour of Wickham. Rejected again by someone he loved in favour of Wickham.

"Who that knows his misfortunes can help feeling an interest in him?"

"His misfortunes! Oh, yes. His misfortunes have been great indeed."

He was pacing around the room, trying to contain himself. It was terrifying the amount of feeling this woman could elicit from him whether it was frustration, love or anger. A man should not live like this. He began to think she did him quite a favour by refusing him.

"And of your infliction! You have reduced him to his current level of poverty!"

Elizabeth continued to throw attacks, blaming him for Wickham's lack of income, as though a steward's son would normally deserve much more than a commission in the militia at any rate. Darcy loved her, but her feelings of generosity were severely misplaced at times.

"This is your opinion of me! Thank you for explaining my faults so fully! But perhaps these offences might have been overlooked had not your pride been hurt by my honest confessions. If I concealed my struggle and flattered you, I suppose you would have suppressed these accusations. But I am not ashamed of what I related. Could you expect me to rejoice in the inferiority of your connections? To congratulate myself on the hope of relations whose condition in life is so decidedly beneath my own?"

He knew now she was vain. He had thought her nearly without fault—except for being too kind—but if she was so charmed by Wickham then it was obvious what would have swayed her opinion. He would not have it. What a fool he was to wish for her! He offered honesty and respect and she wanted flattery and deceit.

"You are mistaken, Mr. Darcy, if you suppose that the mode of your declaration affected me in any other way than as it spared me the concern which I might have felt in refusing you, had you behaved in a more gentlemanlike manner."

He was not gentlemanly? He could scarcely believe her words.

"You could not have made the offer of your hand in any possible way that would have tempted me to accept it."

Impossible. Absolutely impossible. She had refused him. She did not love him; she did not esteem him, and she found him no gentleman. She had no mercy and continued speaking.

"From the very beginning—from the first moment, I may almost say—of my acquaintance with you, your manners, impressing me with the fullest belief of your arrogance, your conceit, and your selfish disdain of the feelings of others, were such as to form the groundwork of an immovable dislike. I had not known you a month before I felt that you were the last man in the world whom I could ever be prevailed on to marry."

The shredded remnants of his pride demanded he pull himself together. "You have said quite enough, madam. I perfectly comprehend your feelings, and have now only to be ashamed of what my own have been. Forgive me for having taken up so much of your time, and accept my best wishes for your health and happiness."

He hastily left the room, angry at Elizabeth, at George Wickham, Charles Bingley, Jane Bennet and whoever else had given her such a false impression of him. Mostly though, he was angry at himself. He was nothing more than a ridiculous boy again, mooning over a pretty pair of eyes in a woman who lacked not only all sense and wisdom, but any modicum of civility and compassion. He would be her fool no more.

Elizabeth collapsed into sobs as Mr. Darcy left. It was beyond her understanding entirely. She had received an offer of marriage from Mr. Darcy! That he would love her enough to propose when his own arguments against his friend's alignment with his sister must be even more keenly felt for himself. She did wish she had behaved more civilly, although she could not repent refusing him. Upon hearing the sounds of a carriage, knowing it was the Collinses and Maria arriving home, she dashed upstairs to her room.

Upon waking, her thoughts turned to the same subject as they did the evening before. Mr. Darcy loved her, and nothing could be the same in the world ever again. She chose to go for a long walk lest she question too much how his stares and silence were a sign for love, and wonder how Mr. Bingley's open admiration for her sister was not. She had always known there were people with different dispositions in the world, but could love be so differently expressed? She shook her head. It mattered not. He would soon recover from his infatuation, and soon she would be at Longbourn where life may pass another twenty years without so much upsetting her ways as the arrival of two gentleman to Netherfield Park had done the previous autumn. And good riddance at that!

She chose a different path than usual, hoping to not encounter Mr. Darcy, but too late she recognised his form. She tried to turn as though she did not see him, but he had suddenly noticed her. A sad mirror of their acquaintance.

"Miss Bennet!" he called, and she had no choice but to face him.

"Mr. Darcy," she replied.

"Would you do me the honour of reading this letter?"

She took it but looked at it with resignation. She had thought he would leave immediately, but he quickly explained to her:

"It is not another proposal, if that is what you think, and you likely do, as vain as you are."

"Good day, Mr. Darcy!" She shoved the letter back into his hands and turned, but he caught her arm.

"I only wanted to explain myself about Bingley." He pushed the letter back in her hands.

"If you have a defence why not say so last night?"

"Good God, Elizabeth! I had proposed marriage to you. I declared, in passionate terms, that I love you and you rejected me, and you think that then I would be master of myself to inquire calmly as to your misapprehension of my interference between Bingley and your sister? Do you know anything of love? Anything at all?"

He tossed his hands in the air and turned his face from her. His profile was a handsome one but marred with pain and regret, ashen from lack of sleep. She could at least have sympathy on him.

"I am sorry for your pain and for my loss of temper yesterday. You are correct, though; I do not know what it is like to be in love and honestly have no faith in men's affections lasting."

He sighed at her words. Hopefully, he understood that she did not doubt merely his affection.

"We are so alike," he said sorrowfully.

She wanted to lighten the mood, although she could not understand why she remained at all. "You also distrust men's constancy? You see, you have already overcome your foolishness. In time, you may allow yourself to laugh over it."

He turned a tortured expression on her and spoke lowly. "You are quite mistaken. I do not doubt men's affections, or mine for you at least. I had never thought much of a woman's constancy, and now I do pray I am correct, and you will soon forget him."

She bristled at his reprimanding tone. She had already showed him more kindness than he deserved. "You said I was under a misapprehension about Mr. Bingley?"

"You seem to believe I did some kind of evil to separate your sister and my friend. I did not inform Bingley she was in town; that was all. I was first told by you she planned to stay several weeks and then I heard from Miss Bingley, as she had received a note from Miss Bennet. Miss Bingley expected a call from your sister and, in a conversation with my own sister, she confessed that Miss Bennet had not called."

Elizabeth gasped and stepped backwards. "No! Jane called on Miss Bingley right away. The call was not returned for over a month, and not even a note came in between!"

Darcy was quiet for a moment, clearly thinking through her claims. "I regret to say it would not surprise me if Miss Bingley used deception and discouraged the friendship. She would not have wanted Miss Bennet to call when Bingley was at home."

"He does not stay with you?"

"No, why should he?"

Elizabeth let out a frustrated sigh. "More lies. Tell me, is he nearly engaged to your sister?"

Darcy's face took on a hard look. "My sister is only fifteen. She is not receiving suitors for several more years."

"Do you desire a match between them?"

He paused and Elizabeth perceived he would rather not admit the fact. "If they both wished it, I could not ask for a better husband for my sister. Bingley is not ready to settle to marriage now, but once his mind is made I know he would be a constant and loving spouse. They are alike in many ways as well. But that would be several years away. I swear, I have never separated Bingley from a woman based on my own motivation."

"But you have interfered with him before!"

"He attracts certain ladies, usually. He is blinded by their beauty and does not see their shallowness, their want of character and, often, their clearly-mercenary ways."

She considered Colonel Fitzwilliam's words again. Mr. Darcy and Mr. Bingley had spent the summer together and yet they did not arrive at Netherfield until the autumn.

"Would you have done more to separate Jane from Mr. Bingley?" She could hardly understand why she needed to know.

"In the past I have only needed to suggest he leave the lady's presence long enough to reconsider. He would inevitably then meet another lady, and his infatuation with the first one quickly ended convincing me that his attachment was transitory."

She nodded her head. Yes, Bingley was easily inconstant but Darcy had said he knew his own affections were different. She wanted to ask him how he could be so certain but knew that would be cruel and impertinent. Instead, she straightened her shoulders.

"Thank you for explaining, Mr. Darcy. I believe you have acquitted yourself of harming my sister."

"I must confess I did not perceive affection from her, but you must be more certain than I in this case. I do apologise she was disappointed by Bingley."

They awkwardly stood before each other. A new thought entered her mind, but she knew not if she was brave enough to voice it. However, she knew she must be fair to him, and to know for herself.

"Did-did-did you have any other defences left unsaid last night?" She held her breath.

He looked at her for a long moment, his eyes searching hers. She knew she could not return his love, but she still wished to sketch his character. This would be her last chance to do so. She had thought he looked at her in contempt, but he looked at her with admiration. Her understanding of his character was more incomplete than she thought.

"Do you understand what you are asking, Elizabeth?" he asked softly.

She blushed and turned her eyes when she saw the longing and hope in his. "I...never mind, it was wrong of me to ask."

"But you believed him so willingly. You wanted to think the worst of me. You are so ready to give your heart to anyone but me."

"You are incorrect, sir. I have given my heart to no one. Forgive me. I am too much like my father. I only wanted to understand your character."

"I thought you did understand! I thought you knew."

"Knew what?"

"Knew me! Knew that I loved you! Knew that Wickham was at best a liar and not to be trusted. And I thought I knew you."

"How...how would I know Mr. Wickham is not to be trusted? What proof do you have that you will not tell me?"

"I suggested twice that you ask your uncle about the ability to ignore wills. I do not know what Wickham has precisely accused me of. I can only surmise it is about the living he was meant to receive."

"I thought you were mocking my relations and boasting of your triumph over Mr. Wickham!"

"What have I done to make you think this? When have I mocked you? While I know I pained you yesterday, my objections were sound and would not just affect me, but you needed to be aware for your own good as well! Do you not consider society might reject you because of your relations? What they may even believe of you for my interest? Had I been less selfish I never would have proposed at all!"

She took another step backwards. He was concerned for her reputation when he had said society would think he was a fool to marry her. How could she have been so naive? No, she had never questioned if society would accept her providing her husband did. And what of Jane? She likely would have faced similar prejudices. If Bingley was not certain of his love for her, then it would be cruel to make her go through so much, only to find he had lost his affection for her. Could Darcy have even been considering Jane's sensibilities then?

Other than his first comments on her looks had she ever known him to mock her? Or did she just assume he did because he was so wealthy and mighty, and Miss Bingley's dislike was so plain? He clearly thought better of his first assessment of her, she should move beyond those words as well. When she did, she reconsidered many things she had thought she understood of the man.

She stepped forward and clutched his arms. "Tell me, tell me what Mr. Wickham has done!"

"We should walk as I explain." He offered her his arm, and she took it with little thought.

As they walked Darcy explained how Wickham turned down the living provided for him in his godfather's will. He asked instead for additional money to study law, and promptly gambled it away. Then, when the living he declined fell open, he asked for placement. When Darcy would not give it, deeming him already recompensed and grossly unfitted for a pastoral role, Wickham turned hateful and abused him verbally as frequently as possible. She did not realise how her hand unconsciously squeezed his arm tighter.

He ceased walking, and she looked up at him, finally seeing him in a respectful light.

"You should not blame yourself for being deceived by him."

"You are too kind. You certainly tried to tell me, but I was too prejudiced."

"Last night I was bitter and angry with your response, but as I thought over matters, I began to consider your words. From the first moment of our acquaintance, I did behave poorly—long before you supposed I separated Bingley and your sister and before you met Wickham. You have already reprimanded me for not dancing at the assembly. From then on I surely appeared haughty and proud—again you attempted to reprimand me months ago."

She held her breath, praying he would not mention his words at the assembly—or any of her saucy speeches—which she so desperately wished to ignore her own weakness of character exposed by them. He paused only for a moment and then continued.

"I gave you every reason to doubt me. And Wickham has deceived many. I...I have more to tell you. I should have found a way to warn the area when I knew he arrived, although I was uncertain he would remain, or how to explain it."

She only nodded her head and furrowed her brow, hardly supposing what could be more serious.

"Last summer Wickham intruded on my notice again. My sister was taken from school and placed in the care of a companion. They were to summer at Ramsgate. Wickham met her there, I know now he had a past friendship with Georgiana's companion, it was all by design. He convinced Georgiana he was in love with her, and she with him, and to consent to an elopement. She is to inherit thirty thousand pounds.

"I arrived a day before, by the merest chance. Actually, because of Bingley. We had visited a friend's estate, and he soon became enamoured with the friend's sister. I suggested we leave early to allow him to think about matters. I arrived at Ramsgate unexpectedly and there my sister confessed her engagement," he spat the words, "to me. Wickham left immediately; never to even speak to her again. She was heartbroken."

"How dreadful for your sister."

"Yes, she took it very hard and is still convinced she would have brought shame to the Darcy name. We...we were raised to take that very seriously."

Elizabeth nodded her head. Of course, he would hope for a better match than her. She released his arm and walked a few paces away, her back facing him. She heard him approach behind her.

"It is understandable you did not specifically address the topic in Hertfordshire. You would not wish to cast suspicion on your sister's reputation. Besides we have no rich ladies. Well, Mary King has recently inherited ten thousand pounds..."

"I am afraid that would be tempting enough to him in his current situation. But I worried because I am certain he also wanted revenge on me."

"Why should that matter in Hertfordshire?"

"Elizabeth," he said and she wondered when she had accepted he had a right to use her Christian name. He had done so several times, and she never corrected him or balked at it.

She turned to face him, confused with some change in the gravity of the moment.

"I wanted to keep you safe, to caution you, but also not to make you an obvious target for his ill will."

She suddenly realised so much. How truly wicked Darcy believed Wickham to be but would not completely describe to a lady; and how much he had cared for her even then. Since his unexpected proposal, she had presumed it only a flight of fancy due to boredom. He professed to care for her for several months, but she had seen no proof during that time. Now, better informed, she could accept even his leaving as proof of his regard. Her heart lurched at the idea of being in his care and protection. The feeling of loneliness eased, and she was tempted by a spark of madness to request he offer his hand again, but she suppressed it.

"Thank you for telling me," she said softly. "I...I think I know you better now."

"And I know you better now."

"Oh yes, vain and simple-minded creature that I am."

He extended his hand and nearly touched her face before dropping it limply to his side. "No, never that. Forgive me. I was angry at myself more than you. Your complaints are just. I have appeared haughty and arrogant, and I would never wish for you to accept me for anything less than love."

Her heart actually ached as though it was pierced and in its pain it cried out to her that she should accept him now. Not today, her mind replied, everything is too new.

"Then...then do we say goodbye now?"

He visibly swallowed, but his eyes never left hers. "How am I supposed to give up trying? I know not how to go on. Loving you has become a part of who I am."

She trembled, longing to give in to the love he still offered. "Nothing has changed, you know. My mother's family still comes from trade. My nearest relations still behave poorly. Society may still shun me."

"Nothing has changed," he said with disaffected calmness. "Good day, Miss Bennet."

He turned and walked away, leaving her alone and astonished. She had not meant to discourage him entirely, to make him think nothing had changed in her regard for him. She watched his back for a moment knowing she had lost her chance forever. Gently-bred ladies do not race after men and declare newly-born sentiments and demand they propose; nor do men of such pride and sense propose to a lady who so callously spurned their first attempt.

She looked down to the letter still in her hand and traced her name on the envelope. There was no reason to keep it now, she had heard all his confessions and believed him among the best of men. Refusing to weep she simply sat on the ground, not caring it was slightly wet from the dew still. She tore open Darcy's letter. It simply said:

Forgive me. I love you.

She could contain the tears no longer.

Chapter

4

Darcy turned and left Elizabeth's side, as she so clearly wanted. He could not say good bye to her. He numbly walked back to the Parsonage and said good bye to the residents and then returned to his aunt's house. The Colonel walked with him, and he explained he had news from his solicitor and needed to leave for London immediately. His cousin easily agreed to the new scheme.

Lady Catherine nearly asked why he had not proposed to Anne on yet another visit, but he knew she would never directly ask him. She could only be too aware of the suspicion by this point. Looking to his cousin for the first time, in perhaps years, it occurred to him she may deserve to be privy to his thoughts.

"Anne, can I speak with you privately?"

Colonel Fitzwilliam jumped out of his chair. "I believe we need to leave immediately."

"It will not take long."

Lady Catherine had been muted by astonishment but was soon pushing everyone out of the room. As he shook his head, the vision of Mrs. Bennet appeared and he wondered how pretentious he must have appeared to Elizabeth to criticise her family when his own behaved similarly.

Anne sat in her chair, her hands clenched tightly together. Perhaps if he was not so acquainted with what a refusal looked like he would not have noticed how terrified his cousin looked.

"Have no fear. I am not proposing."

Her head snapped up, and she asked in a trembling voice. "You are not?"

"No. I have evaded your mother's suggestions for years and will likely continue to do so, but I thought you should know my decision."

"I had thought this year you would cease avoiding the conversation, but for another reason entirely."

He looked at her quizzically.

"I am not blind, Fitzwilliam. Were you too proud to ask her?"

He smiled sadly. Perhaps if he had shown Elizabeth his admiration more she would have accepted him, or at the very least discouraged him. No, he could not wish for either situation. For her to accept him out of gratitude would never be enough, nor could he repent her refusal. He had learned much about himself and at the very least attempted to love her as she deserved.

"No, I asked. She refused."

"She refused?"

Anne's astonishment annoyed rather than soothed him. "She has more integrity than anyone I have met. She does not want my money or connections and was convinced, very rightly so, that I lack a quality of character."

"She must be mistaken somehow."

"No." He could talk of this no more. "I...I do not know what the future holds for me, but I do hope you can find peace and happiness. If you would prefer, I could tell your mother my long-held resolve."

"I have no desire to marry. While she believes she has a claim on you it avoids the concern of finding other suitors."

"If you like. I might suggest avoidance is not always the best tactic."

"You have made up your mind then?"

"On what?"

"Her relations live in London. She will be in London. You can choose either to avoid her or court her good opinion."

"I must give her credit to know her own mind, Anne."

She smiled at his words. "But a woman's mind is not immoveable."

He could never deserve Elizabeth, it would be foolish to try again but Anne seemed disinclined to understand. "I should go. I wish you well."

"Safe travels, Fitzwilliam."

He squeezed her hand and then walked to the door. Lady Catherine nearly fell onto the floor, and Colonel Fitzwilliam was just outside the frame as well. Raising an eyebrow at them both he looked to his cousin. "Is the carriage ready?"

"Yes…"

Lady Catherine interrupted. "Surely you will not be leaving Rosings now!"

"I do regret needing to depart today, but so we must."

He boarded the carriage, and as it passed the Parsonage he could not help glancing at it, wondering where Elizabeth was, how she was feeling and feeling a stab of pain at leaving her presence again.

The very next day the Parsonage party was invited to dine at Rosings. Elizabeth could not see Lady Catherine without wondering how the lady would have behaved upon presentation of Elizabeth as a future niece. The great lady bemoaned the loss of her nephews and added:

"They were excessively sorry to go! But so they always are. The dear Colonel rallied his spirits tolerably till just at last; but Darcy seemed to feel it most acutely; more, I think, than last year. His attachment to Rosings certainly increases."

She glanced at Anne, and Elizabeth could not help but feel envy. Surely he did not actually propose to Anne so immediately after declaring nearly undying love to herself, though. Undoubtedly, if Anne and Darcy were actually engaged Lady Catherine would be regaling them with the announcement. But did he speak with her? Give her a reason to hope? Of course Anne would hope for him. What woman would not wait years in hopes of an honourable and handsome gentleman? She would wait for him. *No*, she told herself. *No, it could not be called waiting when you once refused him.*

"Miss Bennet, you seem out of spirits this evening," Lady Catherine commanded her attention.

"Forgive me, your ladyship. I am still recovering from my headache of last night."

"I think you do not wish to return home so soon. I have told Mrs. Collins I expected you to remain for two months complete. Surely Mrs. Bennet can spare you another fortnight."

"My father cannot, however, and I believe we ought to abide by the original plan and arrive in town next Saturday."

Lady Catherine again attempted to persuade Elizabeth to remain longer, but at last accepted Elizabeth's refusals. She then had many more questions, and copious advice, nay instructions, about the journey, and Elizabeth was thankful she had reason to pay attention. Her mind desired to wander, but it was not safe to reflect in the company of so many others.

In her time remaining at Kent, she indulged in many solitary walks. She found herself recounting Mr. Darcy's last words to her, their final conversation, and she frequently pulled out his simple letter which she carried with her everywhere. At times, she convinced herself she entirely imagined her change of feelings toward the man. One conversation and the knowledge of his innocence in regards to both Jane and Mr. Wickham could not entirely undo all of her previous dislike, could it? But deeper down her heart knew the truth. Their many conversations she now took in a different light.

She considered, too, his words on her vanity. He spoke them in anger and bitterness, but they were true. She thought well of her own opinion, and every successive fault she imagined in Darcy supported the prejudice she formed against him on the night of their first acquaintance. Nor was she immune to Wickham's preference to her. She was embarrassed by her behaviour and words to Darcy. From the beginning, she had always tried to provoke and pain him.

She considered all the things she would rather do differently, but then would resolve it was just as well she would never see him again. Nothing has changed; she repeated to herself over and over again. She had rejected his suit and must now abide by her decision. He would not renew it, her words could not be undone. Meeting again could only bring pain and misery, perhaps to them both, and she could not wish for it. But her spirits were so depressed she could not even appear tolerably cheerful.

On the morning she departed for London, Mr. Collins drew her aside in one final effort to inspire regret or envy in her. Amidst his prattle, he said something which particularly caught her attention. "My dear Charlotte and I have but one mind and one way of thinking. There is in everything a most remarkable resemblance of character and ideas between us. We seem to have been designed for each other."

Elizabeth could hardly suppose such was the case with Charlotte and Mr. Collins yet it might have been for her and Darcy. "We are so alike," he had said. But these regrets would not do. It could only bring heartbreak for her, and she was soon to see Jane, who would need all her attention.

During the journey, Maria rambled on about all the times they had been invited to Rosings and the stories she would have to retell. Elizabeth could only consider what she would have to conceal, even from her dearest Jane.

Jane looked well, although Elizabeth felt she barely got to study her with all the activity Mrs. Gardiner had planned for the ladies on their brief stay.

On her third evening in London, they attended a play. For reasons Elizabeth still did not wish to think about, she found it dull. It was as though only part of her was aware of anything going on.

During the interval between acts, they went to retrieve refreshments and were greeted by some acquaintances of her uncle. A Mr. Johnson was introduced to Elizabeth. He seemed amiable and had many clever things to say about the play. She had rather wished to not meet with anyone and kept attempting to defer to her aunt or Jane, but he seemed to direct his comments to her directly. When she was finally readying for bed, Jane spoke to her.

"Mr. Johnson seemed very interested in you, Lizzy. I think if we were to remain here a few more weeks he would ask to call."

She sighed. Did Jane still hope to meet with Bingley? "Would you rather stay longer? I am certain we need only ask."

Jane shook her head. "No, I am resolved to return home. Mamma may fuss over me, but I am tired of London. I only thought you may wish for some amusements and, if you attract the eye of an amiable and handsome suitor, then we should hardly discourage that."

"Oh, do not think of me. You are by far the prettiest of us and the sweetest tempered. You will surely marry first, and if I have very good luck then I may meet another Mr. Collins in time though truthfully I expect to be a doting aunt and spoil your children. No, I wish to return to Longbourn, to our family and to my gardens." To where I belong and among people who do not expect good behaviour from us.

Jane allowed the topic to drop, and the sisters soon fell asleep.

That same evening Darcy paced the floor of his study. He held a letter he received two days ago from his cousin Anne in one hand. The paper was nearly balled together in his fist.

> She is to depart for London tomorrow and will have arrived by the time you read this. In case you do not know, her relatives are Mr. and Mrs. Gardiner of Gracechurch Street, near Cheapside. I believe she is only to remain for a few days.

> She has been very subdued, seemingly full of regret. I do not think she suffers from implacable resentment as you do. I am my mother's daughter and so I feel compelled to add: it is ungentlemanly of you to not call on an acquaintance when you know of her

presence, and it is terrible that you may be the cause for her lack of spirits and yet you seek no way to ease her sufferings.

The last line angered Darcy each time he read it. Her mother's daughter indeed! He did pause over her reprimand on gentlemanly behaviour. It was so close to Elizabeth's own admonishment, and while her statements were built on faulty beliefs, he had later the same night she said them determined she was correct. It was a true gentleman's duty to put others at ease, and he only ever thought of himself. But this was the raw of it. He knew Elizabeth would not wish to see him. It may be society's mandate to call on acquaintances, but it would be selfish and ungentlemanly to impose his presence on Elizabeth. Lord knew how much he wanted to see her again. He had imagined her as a beautiful flower, his for the taking but too late learned he must be the attentive gardener, who approached with humility and reverence, to know how to secure its bloom.

His hand tightened around the crumpled paper. How did Anne propose he ease Elizabeth's sufferings? What was she suffering from? That her sister was cast aside by Bingley? He thought to their last conversation, even as the memory brought pain. Elizabeth forgave him of his involvement. Did she wish for Miss Bennet to have another chance to meet with Bingley? He could think of no other way that he was the cause of Elizabeth's lack of spirits.

It was difficult to imagine her behaving so in any case. His own melancholy was due to regrets. He had believed he was not a vain man—he had told himself he cared little for what the world thought of him. He knew himself to be good, but he had no humility. He never considered how others felt, how he made others feel. If he held prejudices about how those with less wealth and rank than him behaved, then surely they held prejudices about the rich. They likely thought all rich men and women like his aunt, and he gave the populace of Meryton—and perhaps most places he visited— little reason to think otherwise.

He felt at every turn he had made a mess of things with Elizabeth Bennet; constantly leaving things undone. Even in their last conversation she had asked if it was good-bye for them and he had not the strength to say the words.

In exasperation, he ripped the letter in two, then tore it again and again. Finally, he was left with only fragments of the letter. Breathing heavily after his savage display he deposited them in the rubbish bin. He thought he had finally bested Anne's words when the final piece of the letter fluttered down. *Sufferings.* It glared at him and accused him.

His jaw clenched, and he considered again his cousin's remonstrances. How dare she be so officious as to suggest he visit Elizabeth? How dare she assume she understood Elizabeth's feelings more than he did! And how dare she imply Elizabeth was suffering because of him; because of how he left things. The only thing that could concern Elizabeth was Bingley not caring enough for her sister.

Pacing once more, he considered his thoughts. He had felt himself exonerated from Elizabeth's charges about his involvement in separating Bingley and Miss Bennet. Now, he paused. Was it officious of him to direct Bingley to follow him so much? How did he presume to know Jane Bennet's feelings? He could think of only one way to ease Elizabeth's suffering, if only he could put his pride aside.

After ordering his carriage to be readied, even at the late hour, he arrived at the Hurst townhouse just before supper was served. They had been to the theatre, and he was invited to enjoy the light repast with them. Afterwards, he asked to speak with Bingley alone. His friend seemed melancholy again but agreed.

"Bingley, I have quite the confession to make and I cannot express enough how sorry I am for my intrusion into your affairs."

Furrowing his brows, his friend asked, "What do you mean?"

"For quite some time now I have had you in leading strings and would direct you whom to talk to, where to go...whom to court...or not."

"I am grateful for your assistance."

"But I have behaved like an overbearing mother. You are capable of making your own decisions, especially in regards to your own happiness, and I have selfishly guided you in certain directions."

"I cannot fathom how your actions have been selfish. Rather, I see you suffer with Caroline's attentions."

Darcy sighed. "I hope not all my actions were due to selfishness but they certainly were last fall."

"We were in Hertfordshire..."

"And there I believe you quite liked Jane Bennet. I had not felt the need to counsel you away from her at the time, your admiration seemed no deeper than usual and once in town you seemed in no hurry to return to Netherfield. But as I consider things now, I believe I did you a disservice. I saw you throwing yourself into events with fervour, and I wonder if it was in an attempt to forget Miss Bennet."

Bingley was silent for a long moment before answering very quietly. "You are correct."

"I did not think it at the time, but it makes sense. It is what I always suggested you do when you admired a lady before. Only tell me why you decided she would not suit."

"You and Caroline made no secret how you found her family and connections."

Darcy cringed; it was as he feared. "I was not as vocal as your sister but I did share her concerns."

"I must say it is the first time you did not suggest such things to me. I had supposed you hoped I could make the decision on my own this time. I did not let you down, my friend."

Darcy's heart broke a little at the pride in Bingley's tone. He resolved to confess all. "Perhaps I did, but mostly I was quieter than usual about the matter because I struggled with my own feelings for Miss Elizabeth."

"Elizabeth Bennet! Elizabeth 'not handsome enough to tempt you' Bennet?"

"Yes, although I assure you I soon found her more tempting than any other woman I have met."

"Darcy..."

"What do you take me for? I proposed marriage to her!"

"What? When?"

He let out a deep sigh. "I met with her in Kent again. Her friend in Hertfordshire, Miss Lucas, had married her cousin, Mr. Collins—who you will recall is my aunt's reverend. She was visiting Mrs. Collins. I had tried for all the months we were in town to forget her, to overcome my feelings and I could not. I decided to risk Society's ire."

Bingley's face could not be more surprised. It wounded Darcy to realise his best friend thought him incapable of overcoming his prejudice for love. He recovered soon enough and muttered a congratulations.

Smiling sadly, Darcy replied, "I thank you, but there are no congratulations in order. She refused me."

Again, Bingley showed shock, although less than before. Evidently Elizabeth's dislike had been observed by Bingley.

"I deserved it. She was under some misinformation from Mr. Wickham—he is more wicked than I have told you—but even still, I did not behave in a gentlemanly manner. I had concealed my regard, maintained my reserve and appeared haughty and above my company. She knew nothing good of me, and I arrogantly assumed there was little need to court her or earn her good opinion."

Bingley did not reply and instead looked at the glass in his hand, so Darcy continued. "She also believed I kept you from declaring your love to her sister."

Darcy observed his friend's absorption of that news. His grip on the drink tightened, and his face paled a little.

"She is wrong, of course. You barely said a thing to me."

"Yes, but I am the one who hammered the methods in your head."

"I am my own man!" Bingley cried.

"Bingley...I wonder if there was a point where it would have been worth it to you to follow your heart. For myself, when I believed Miss Elizabeth returned my affections, I was resolved regardless of the logical arguments."

"I think you are right...I sometimes fear that a lady will come to feel true attachment to me, and I will propose out of mere gratitude."

Shaken by his friend's confession, Darcy nearly confessed his knowledge of Jane's feelings but remained silent.

Bingley asked nervously, "Why are you telling me this?"

"Because I have recently been reminded it is ungentlemanly to not call when an acquaintance of yours is in town. Miss Elizabeth is visiting her relatives on her way home from Kent. I also know Miss Bennet is there as well. I have known her to be in town since January."

"You never mentioned a thing!"

"Miss Elizabeth told me she planned to come. Later Miss Bingley spoke with my sister about it. Miss Bennet even called on your sisters, although I did not know of it until the other week. I have learned the civility was not returned for over a month."

"A month!"

"Yes. And again I apologise for my intrusion. For not only should I have called since I knew of her presence, I should have shared that information with you as an acquaintance of theirs, in any case. I was not much worried about your own ability to meet with Miss Bennet. I selfishly wanted to avoid any mention of any Bennet."

"Again I ask why you are telling me this now."

It brought unimaginable pain to think it, but Darcy knew what he must do. He always followed his duty. "I intend to call on Miss Bennet and Miss Elizabeth tomorrow, and I wanted to know if you would like to come."

Bingley was silent for a very long time. He stared at something in the room, or perhaps at nothing at all, but Darcy could not scrutinise the emotion on his friend's face.

At last he replied. "No, I am certain too much time has passed by."

The two gentlemen sat in silence for a moment before Bingley mentioned he was tired, and Darcy bid him good night. On the way back to his own house, he could not understand Bingley's lack of interest in at least seeing Jane again. That was when he realised he could never give up Elizabeth.

The next morning Jane took the Gardiner children on a walk in a park with their governess. They wished to see some of the flowers in one of Elizabeth's books. Elizabeth herself pleaded a headache and sat in the drawing room. She had no desire to see foreign flowers. Only the comfort of those at home could appeal to her. Instead, she attempted to read a book but stared longingly at her letter. Mrs. Gardiner had been speaking with the housekeeper when she suddenly came in the room.

"Elizabeth, there is a caller here to see you."

Worried it was Mr. Johnson she tried to beg off. "Oh, please, Aunt. My head truly does ache."

"Elizabeth Bennet, if you think I am going to turn away Mr. Darcy of Pemberley simply because you took a dislike to him then I can see why your mother bemoans her nerves!"

She stood at her aunt's words and soon Darcy was shown in and after the necessary civilities, they all sat. He was quite attentive to Mrs. Gardiner, which Elizabeth truly appreciated.

"My purpose for calling today was to see if it would meet with Miss Elizabeth and Miss Bennet's agreement to be introduced to my sister before they are to leave town."

Mrs. Gardiner looked to Elizabeth with raised eyebrows. She blushed but replied, "I can speak for Jane when I say we would like that. I enjoyed hearing about your sister when we were in Kent. I hope you found her well."

"Very, thank you."

"Elizabeth, you did not mention you had seen Mr. Darcy again while in Kent," said Mrs. Gardiner.

"Oh? I did not mean to exclude it. Yes, his aunt is Mr. Collins's patroness. He and his cousin visited, and we met many times." She gave a weak smile.

Mrs. Gardiner looked between the two and, with tact only slightly better than Mrs. Bennet, recalled that she had been meeting with the housekeeper on a serious matter and if they would please excuse her for just a moment.

Elizabeth closed her eyes and blushed again.

Darcy cleared his throat. "What were you reading?"

"A report of the latest news from the African Association." She admired the society not only for the quest of natural knowledge, such as the source of the Niger River, but also for its stance against slavery.

She was unsurprised when he asked to see it; they really were quite alike. Without thought, she handed the book to him to peruse but at the last moment remembered her letter was in it. Attempting to pull it back, the book fell to the ground, and the letter fluttered out. Elizabeth jumped out of her chair, and Darcy immediately stooped to collect the book and letter, but when he saw his handwriting on the paper he snatched his fingers away as though burned.

Elizabeth saw it all with mortified resignation. She looked away entirely uncertain what to do. In the eternity that passed between two heartbeats, she heard him step toward her.

"Elizabeth?" he said it so reverently, and she had been so certain she would only ever hear harshness from him that a tear slid down her cheek. She still could not look at him, though.

"Elizabeth, I did not come to ask if you desired to meet Georgiana."

"Oh, of course if you have thought better of it…"

"No, I still wish for you to meet her but, as I have always wished, as her sister."

She spun to face him then.

"My affections and wishes are unchanged. They will never change, but one word from you will silence me…"

"Yes."

He blinked in surprise, and she said again what her heart had been screaming at her to utter since their walk the morning after his proposal.

"Yes, I wish to marry you."

He looked guarded but spoke quietly. "You kept my letter."

"I carry it with me everywhere."

He began to smile. "Dare I hope you have found a reason to esteem me?"

She nodded her head. "I have found many reasons to love you."

Suddenly she was in his arms. She gasped in surprise, and her senses were filled with him. His clean scent, his strong arms, the powerful beat of his heart.

"I love you so ardently, my lovely Elizabeth, my own Lizzy."

She smiled at his endearments. How had she tried to deny herself this?

She spoke into his chest. "What made you seek me out? I thought you were resolved to give me up. I did not mean that I had not changed my opinion of you. Only that your objections were still present."

He pulled her back to look her in the eye. "I tried again to give you up but could not. I told you that loving you had become a way of life for me. Nor were those my objections. They were what I anticipated Society's to be. If I could not overcome them, then I should not offer for you. I was certain of my choice."

She tightened her hold on his waist, slightly amazed at how bold and unrestrained she felt. "I wanted to accept you by then. I was only afraid of my own feelings."

He chuckled, and she loved hearing the rumble of it. "I told you we were very alike."

"I like thinking that. You need someone to think more like you than the friends you have do."

"And you need someone that thinks more like you than your family and friends do."

She squeezed him tighter. "You really did understand me."

"No, I did not consider how I appeared to you. How proud and arrogant I was. I was so blithely confident that I never once thought you would refuse me; that although embarrassed by your family you would defend them. I understood parts of you, but not the whole."

She laughed. "You certainly understood more of me than I did of you!"

"But I understand myself more now and that is because of you as well."

"You will not allow me to take the greater share of the blame?"

"Never!"

She smiled broadly, and his eyes travelled to her lips. Their banter ended, and she wondered how it was she had been in his arms so long without kissing to begin with.

"Lizzy…" he said in a low voice.

"Yes." She replied and tilted her face up.

"Truly?"

"Yes, I want..."

She closed her eyes as she felt his head descend. Finally, his lips brushed against hers. They were so soft, so smooth. He continued with several more light kisses before deepening it. The bang of the front door and the voices of little children registered in her mind. They had just reluctantly separated when Jane stuck her head in the room.

"Mr. Darcy!"

Her eyes flicked between the two and Elizabeth knew she would have to explain all to her sister. She only wondered what to say about Bingley. She had not talked with Darcy about the matter.

Jane sat with them for several minutes until Darcy declared he must leave. Elizabeth walked him to the door, her aunt still suspiciously absent.

"What will I tell Jane? I do not wish to upset her but…"

"But?"

"I will not turn away my own happiness simply because your friend broke my sister's heart."

He smiled at the strength of her determination. "I am sorry, Elizabeth. I did call on him and attempted to explain matters.

I did not reveal your sister's feelings to him, but I told him the alteration in my feelings of an alliance with your family."

"What did he say?"

"He did not think it necessary to call on Miss Bennet as she had been in town so long and was soon to depart. I was surprised at his decision, but I do not know his heart, other than he would never hurt a lady by design."

"I agree. Perhaps it is simply something time took care of. Young couples are frequently separated by some means and their affection wanes." He gave her a look she could not quite make out, but interpreted it as insecurity. "But not us, sir."

"Sir? Will you not address me as Fitzwilliam when we are in private?"

She smiled shyly but agreed. "But not us, Fitzwilliam. I will not be cast aside by distance or time."

He smiled tenderly at her. "No, I have already tried. After speaking with Bingley, I knew I would never give up trying to win your hand." He kissed her forehead. "I do love you Lizzy."

She smiled at the sweetness of his words. "As I love you, Fitzwilliam."

He kissed her hand and reluctantly departed to his carriage while Elizabeth hoped for the wisdom to explain matters to her sister.

Chapter 5

Jane listened to her sister's story with patience. She tried to be understanding, but it all made so little sense to her.

"You love Mr. Darcy?"

"Yes, is that so hard to believe?"

"Yes, it is! I thought you were quite determined to hate him."

"Determined is the word."

"So you did not hate him?"

"I wanted to. I see now I never really had any reason to dislike him at all."

"You know I never thought Mr. Darcy so deficient in the appearance of goodness. Did you really come to your senses so quickly about him?"

Elizabeth paused and furrowed her brow.

"No, do not keep such a secret from me, Lizzy."

Her sister let out a deep sigh. "Very well. My larger objection to Darcy was because I was convinced he schemed to keep Mr. Bingley in London and later kept your presence in town a secret."

"But Miss Bingley made it clear that her brother knew I was here."

"Apparently Miss Bingley has been the one scheming. She told Darcy's sister that you never called on her."

Jane first felt her blood drain away from her face and then immediately return. "So, Mr. Darcy knew I was in town but it appeared I did not care to keep the acquaintance?"

"Yes..." Elizabeth trailed off, and Jane was certain she was afraid to tell the full truth.

"Tell me all! The worst I can do is think poorly of someone, and you always tell me that I am too generous."

Elizabeth let out an uncomfortable laugh. "Darcy had thought you were indifferent to Mr. Bingley when we were all in Hertfordshire. Charlotte did say to me that she believed you were too reserved, so I suppose I cannot really blame Darcy. I know you can only be yourself. You do not wish for everyone to know your heart but..."

"But?"

"But, I hope it means you really did not feel very much for Mr. Bingley. He hardly seems to deserve you. If he had any true regard for you, surely he would have returned to press his suit and, yet, he chose not to accompany Darcy on his call. Even if he did not feel attached to you, why would he not give you the courtesy of a call, and why would he not return to the estate he has leased?"

"Whatever he feels, do you suspect I did not love him?" How could Elizabeth be so unfeeling?

"I can only hope whatever you feel for Mr. Bingley will soon be forgot and you will soon experience something altogether more pleasing."

"I cannot fathom feeling more for any man than I have ever felt for him," she answered quietly.

"Dearest, I know it is your nature to be quiet, but I believe when you are certain of your love you cannot keep it to yourself."

Jane hastily stood. "I am not like you! There is more than one way to love. Mr. Darcy loved you all along you say, and you never saw it! None of us did."

"Charlotte suspected as much, and we believe even Miss Bingley did."

"Do you hear this 'we' you speak of? How easy it was for you to speak out and confess your feelings when he already made his plain. I did not have that luxury!"

"Jane," Elizabeth said in a soothing voice and took one of her hands. "I do not expect you to behave like me. But I would like you to behave like yourself. You speak your mind when you believe you are correct; you always state your opinions, even if they are too generous. However, whenever we spoke about Mr. Bingley you were guarded, even in your opinions to me. I believe you had reservations. What are you afraid of?"

Elizabeth rose and kissed Jane's cheek. "Enough for now; I will let you rest. Mr. Darcy is calling again tomorrow, and I believe he will wish to accompany us to Longbourn to speak with Father. I do not know if he will stay at Netherfield; we did not get to discuss very much today. I am uncertain if we will have to see Mr. Bingley again soon."

Elizabeth departed to her own room, leaving Jane with many thoughts. She accepted that Elizabeth was correct in one respect. Jane had not acted very much like herself in regards to Mr. Bingley. Why had she tried to protect herself from heartbreak all along? She considered her sister's feelings for Mr. Darcy. Perhaps they were more alike than she had thought. Their behaviour was different, but the cause for their actions were likely the same.

Elizabeth was wrong on one thing, though. Jane truly loved Mr. Bingley even if he did not return her regard. Her affectionate heart could not help but be touched by such attentions from an amiable young man. Perhaps if he were older or had learned greater constancy, she would have been his choice. She contented herself with that thought. Another thing was clear: she would have to attempt to meet with Mr. Bingley as nothing more than an indifferent acquaintance.

The next day Darcy called as Elizabeth predicted, and matters of travelling to Longbourn were settled. To spare the Gardiners, and the Bennets any inconvenience, Elizabeth, Jane and Maria Lucas would travel to Hertfordshire in a Darcy carriage. He would travel next to it on his horse. Uncertain if he would be welcomed to stay at Longbourn, or would need to seek lodgings in Meryton, they would set out early the following day.

No mention was made of Darcy staying at his friend's leased house, and Jane resented the pitying looks she received from Darcy and Elizabeth during the conversation. Even Maria seemed sensible enough to not mention anything about it. She must have looked as fragile as she felt.

During the drive itself, she attempted to not see every time Darcy and Elizabeth shared a smile through the carriage window. She also did not notice when Darcy beamed as Elizabeth put her hand on his arm when they stopped to change the horses. He looked at her like she was a treasure he would always value. And Elizabeth deserved it, of course.

She was not jealous, but the pain of knowing she would never receive such a look from Bingley was acute. Worse still was knowing that there were times when he had smiled upon her as if she were the sunlight in his world. But no more. Whether by design, chance or her own fault she had lost him and held no more hope. For, surely, if he had any desire to meet with her again he would be at his friend's side. Elizabeth insisted Jane would find a greater love, but Jane could not be so optimistic. She had been paraded before men for nearly eight years. In that time, she had had plenty of suitors, but only one evoked true affection from her. She certainly did not have another eight years to be so choosy. She would marry someone; it was her duty. She would be fond of him; she was generally fond of everyone. But no one else could stir her heart. Of that, she had no doubt.

At last they arrived, and she knew she would have too little peace to continue to brood. Mrs. Bennet met them in shocked silence. An express had been sent to Mr. Bennet to apprise him of the change in transportation, but it seemed he did not deem it necessary to share such information with his wife.

Naturally, the silence lasted only momentarily. Jane saw the exact moment Mrs. Bennet considered that Mr. Darcy accompanied them because he desired to court Jane.

"Mr. Darcy," Mrs. Bennet began, "it is always such a pleasure to see you. And how are Mr. Bingley and his sisters and brother?"

"Very well, thank you."

"Thank you so much for accompanying the girls. I did not know you had seen Jane in town." She sent a harsh look Jane's way in silent reprimand for not writing of the non-existent meetings.

"Mr. Darcy actually spent several weeks in Kent, Mamma. I had not seen him at all until a few days ago."

Mrs. Bennet was silent, her brow furrowing. Jane sighed to herself. She thought the trail of evidence obvious enough, but it seemed her mother refused to consider the idea. Darcy interrupted her thoughts.

"I had the very great pleasure of meeting with Miss Elizabeth many times while I visited my aunt. Mr. Collins is her rector."

Mrs. Bennet's eyebrows raised to her hair-line and she nearly shrieked, "You met with Elizabeth?"

It was intended to be a question but sounded more like an accusation to them all.

Darcy cleared his throat and sent the woman a silencing glare. "I would like an audience with Mr. Bennet, ma'am."

"Of course," she said before departing to find a maid, leaving the others to refreshments.

The silence was tense even for the three of them, but it was not long before Darcy was invited to the library.

Mrs. Bennet asked the girls to leave with her. "Girls, you must be exhausted. Come upstairs to freshen up and tell me all about your weeks away."

Elizabeth gave Darcy an encouraging smile as he entered the library before meeting her mother's glare. Jane desired only to have the storm over.

Darcy sat in Mr. Bennet's library and attempted to conceal his anxiety. Elizabeth may have believed Wickham's lies, in part, because he flattered her vanity——he told himself that Wickham only flattered Elizabeth's sense of judgment and not that her beauty felt flattered——but she had disliked him long before meeting Wickham. His offences were many and given broadly to all of the Meryton area. Thus, Darcy felt no small concern that Mr. Bennet may object to their marriage. Any father that could do right by her would care more for the prospective husband's character than his purse.

Mr. Bennet's voice interrupted his thoughts. "I am waiting for you to begin, Mr. Darcy. You requested this meeting. Or was it simply a guise to get away from the ladies? If so, you did not think that through, young man. Mrs. Bennet surely thinks you are asking for one of my daughters' hands."

Darcy cleared his throat. "She would not be incorrect."

Mr. Bennet finally put his book down and leaned over the desk. He raised his eyebrow, similar to Elizabeth, and if Darcy was not mistaken there was a twinkle of amusement in the older gentleman's eyes.

"I believe Jane is taken with another and Lizzy we know you disapprove of. You are stupider than I thought if you wish for any of the younger girls," Mr. Bennet drawled.

Well, at least he was not being tossed out of the house entirely. Suppressing his hurt pride, he humbly stated, "I do not disapprove of her; I greatly admire her. I request Miss Elizabeth's hand in marriage."

He was met with a bark of laughter. After several moments, he was asked by a grinning father, "Have you spoken with her?"

"Yes, I was fortunate enough to gain her acceptance and we wish to marry."

They had not discussed their options should Mr. Bennet refuse. He did not even know when she came of age. Actually, there were many things he did not know. Their entire courtship was haphazard, and many things left undone and unsaid.

Mr. Bennet turned serious. "When...when have you even seen Elizabeth again?"

"I have been in Kent, visiting my aunt. She is your cousin's patroness."

"Lizzy was there for six weeks. She made no mention of you."

Darcy glanced to the pile of unopened letters on Mr. Bennet's desk. He had no idea if Elizabeth would have mentioned him in a letter, but she might have noted his arrival. Then again, that likely would not help his situation.

Seeing his glance, Mr. Bennet sorted through the letters and must have found one from Elizabeth. He tore it open.

"You only arrived three weeks ago!" He roared. "Young man! I do not care for your ten thousand a year, and wonder at whatever sort of trickery you have used on my daughter to make her accept a marriage proposal on less than a month's courtship."

Darcy winced. In truth, it was even less time than Mr. Bennet imagined. Darcy avoided Elizabeth entirely the first week he was in the country. He took a deep breath.

"I am not a new acquaintance. I admired your daughter greatly while in Hertfordshire."

"No, you determined her not handsome enough to tempt you and felt the whole community beneath your notice."

Darcy froze. "Someone heard?"

"Elizabeth heard."

My God. A number of things made more sense now. Undone business indeed!

"I see by your countenance you did not know. Elizabeth is...she is special. She is not like most other girls. She laughed at your haughty stupidity, at first."

"I assure you, I understand just what a treasure she is. I have long since been captivated by her beauty, her wit and many other superior qualities. She is unlike any lady I have ever known. While I did not know the source of her first dislike of me, we have discussed the matter. She was rightly angry with me. She was not swayed by either my charm, my connections or my wealth." Lord help him, he would never understand how she came to love him but was grateful for it nonetheless.

Mr. Bennet paused and scrutinised his companion. "She rejected you!"

"Quite soundly." His lips twitched as he tried to contain his smile. "As I said, we have discussed the matter, cleared some misinformation, resolved our difficulties and now she has accepted my hand."

"She so quickly changed her opinion?"

It was a matter Darcy did not like to think on. "You are welcome to speak with her, sir." He certainly needed some reassurances after her father's questions. In another instant, he regretted his suggestion for fear her father would attempt to alter her mind.

"Oh, I will. I fear whatever caused this change in sentiments in my daughter is very new. I can hardly think any man worthy of her but we know nothing good of you and yet in a matter of weeks she is smitten and accepting your proposals … and after rejecting them the first time."

Darcy shifted uncomfortably in his seat. "When I was first in the country we were here only six weeks. It was made known to me then that a proposal from my friend to your eldest daughter would not have been looked upon unfavourably. Indeed, your cousin proposed to Miss Elizabeth off an acquaintance of mere days."

"She told you of that, did she?" She had not, but that was not the point. "Does she fear her mother will find another terrible man for her? Because I supported her against Collins, and I will support her against you!"

"My examples, sir, are merely to show that I do not believe length of the sentiments were a contributing factor in those cases."

"Lizzy is not like Jane. She may feel things very fervently one moment and just as soon as forget them the next." Darcy could not like that illustration of Elizabeth's character at all. "And while Collins tries my patience, I have heard terrible things of you."

So had Wickham told the entire town his lies? It should have discouraged him, but he was pleased it was not a secret for Elizabeth's ears alone. "You speak of Mr. Wickham, I presume. Allow me to settle the matter."

Darcy explained his history with Wickham, sparing no detail. "Obviously, I would ask you keep aspects of this as private as possible."

"It would not do for him to remain in the area with his character unknown."

"I generally think he is no more unscrupulous than some, except for his desire for revenge on me. Wickham is clever enough to realise the militia is a good opportunity—barring the arrival of any wealthy heiress."

"Perhaps, but if you marry Elizabeth then we might become targets."

Blood drained from Darcy's face. He had not recently considered that. More things left undone. All because he was too eager to have Elizabeth.

"You really do care for her?"

"I love her!" Darcy had not meant to declare his sentiments like some kind of love-struck pup, but perhaps it would help his cause. "I now know I have loved her a very long time, even though I first concealed the attraction. I was aware of the arguments my circle would raise against the union. But, with time to consider them properly, my feelings have only strengthened. You must acknowledge she is deserving of my feelings. I am not a green boy infatuated with a silly girl with nothing but a comely face and good nature to recommend her."

"You are fortunate, then, that the militia departs in two weeks. We will announce the engagement then, sir."

Darcy blinked, not even caring that Mr. Bennet smirked. He truly was to marry Elizabeth.

"Now, if you would send Elizabeth to see me. I promise to not keep her long."

Darcy grinned and rose to shake Mr. Bennet's hand. "Anything you wish, sir. Thank you!"

He exited the room and on his way to the drawing room was informed by the housekeeper the ladies were all above stairs. Passing along her father's request, Darcy chose to pace outside while he waited.

Elizabeth hurried to her father's library, wondering if she was still betrothed. There were so many things she needed to discuss with Darcy.

"Papa, you wished to speak with me?"

"Mr. Darcy has asked for your hand and has told me you have even accepted him!"

"It is true."

"Have you not always disliked him?"

"No, I do like him! I love him!"

"Sit down a minute, child. We must discuss this sensibly. Explain your change in sentiments."

Elizabeth blushed and dearly wished she had been more moderate in her earlier expressions. "I have been nonsensical."

Her father only raised an eyebrow.

"I know better than to hold to first impressions and my first impression of him, of course, was that he was too haughty to dance with anyone and specifically did not care if he wounded anyone's feelings—mine in particular. From that moment, I was determined to dislike him at each turn. I even believed Mr. Wickham's words on such a short acquaintance, despite the inappropriateness of his raising the matter, and with no proof."

"Mr. Darcy has explained to me his history with Mr. Wickham."

"Then you know how foolish I have been; how vain I have been. But I would hope you agree with me, such resentment and spite is not usually in my nature."

"No, indeed. I just expressed to Mr. Darcy my concerns for your feelings lasting."

"Papa!" She took a deep breath. Hopefully, her father had not undone everything with Darcy. "I admired him all along.

There were inconsistencies in his character, but I chose not to examine them. How could he debate with me as an equal if he also disdained all of us? He frequently stared at me, asked me to dance several times—what man does that for someone he does not find pretty? Mr. Darcy and I have discussed my misconceptions and his poor manners. We have come to an understanding. If it satisfies him that he has engaged my affections, then you can have no further objections. He will forever treat me with respect and I will be very well settled."

"I have already given my permission, child. I only hoped to be certain of your own feelings."

"I love him because I am assured of his character. He does not shift about and change who he is for the approval of others. He is the same as he always was, only now I understand him better. He has no improper pride. He never despised me for my impertinent behaviour, could there greater proof of his truly amiable nature?" Without waiting for his answer, she pressed on. "He loved me while he was in Hertfordshire. He chose to leave because he thought he had a duty to his family to marry better, and showing me too much attention, despite his efforts, may draw Wickham's notice. His love is not the work of a moment. I refused him, vehemently, but he was so kind. Even when it seemed hopeless, he assured me of his steadfast love."

"If this be the case, he deserves you. I could not have parted with you, my Lizzy, to anyone less worthy. You may go to him now."

After a quick kiss to her father's cheek, she left the room directly. The housekeeper informed her Darcy had gone outside.

"Fitzwilliam?" She found him pacing to the side of the house near her flower garden with the water fountain her mother insisted upon. He spun around at the sound of her voice, an apprehensive smile on his face.

"What did your father say?"

"He gave his blessing, of course."

It seemed those were the words he was waiting to hear for he immediately pulled her into an embrace. They still had much to speak on, but for the moment she could feel his thoughts, his panic.

She pulled back to look him in the eye. "You feared I would reject you again? Do you think I am so inconstant?"

He met her gaze and said, with complete seriousness, as he took her hands in his then led her to a nearby bench. "No. You are the most loyal woman I have ever met. I know what a treasure it is to have your affections. I cannot understand what I have done to change your mind."

"You were simply you."

"Simply me?"

"You are as you ever were. I was always fascinated with you, but blinded by hurt and twisted your every action and word. But I understand your disposition now."

"Still, there is much we do not know of each other. And it seems we must wait another fortnight before enjoying our engagement."

"Father did not mention this to me! Why?"

"We do not wish Wickham to know before I can come up with a permanent solution for him."

Elizabeth smiled. "Actually, Lydia tells me he has gone ahead to Brighton, where the regiment will be decamping to."

"Thank God," he said as he pulled her closer to him. He wrapped his arms around her shoulders. "I finally have you, Lizzy. I was loathe to give you up even for a few weeks."

"I agree, Fitzwilliam."

"Now, I believe we have some unfinished business about our courtship."

"Engagement, I believe."

"But I do intend to court you." He smiled as he pulled her even closer and presented a rose while he looked down to her mouth.

"About this unfinished business?" she whispered, making him lower his head.

"Yes?" he asked and then licked his lips.

"I think it ought to wait for a few minutes." Their lips nearly met.

"No, no it cannot. Not another minute, not another second."

At last his lips met hers again. Elizabeth gave one happy sigh of contentment before entirely different feelings enveloped her. When at last her betrothed pulled back, Elizabeth felt entirely undone.

Chapter 6

October 5, 1812

In the weeks that followed, Darcy and Elizabeth enjoyed a pleasant courtship and grew in their love and confidence in each other. Jane was the dutiful chaperone, and although she could not begrudge Elizabeth happiness, she could not help but feel the sadness at her own situation. Fortunately for Darcy's peace of mind Wickham managed an elopement with a wealthy heiress he met in Brighton. More fortunately for the lady, her godfather, as Wickham discovered to his horror was a powerful man with connections in criminal enterprises who kept her interests at heart. If Wickham neglected his bride, sought to blackmail or harm Darcy or anyone else, he would meet a foul end.

Just as Darcy and Elizabeth's happiness seemed complete, Jane's ended. Just before the wedding Bingley was called to oversee some interests of his in the Indies. He would not return for a year. If ever Jane held hope of meeting him again and gaining his affections, they died with the news. She thought her heart itself had died when news came that he had a serious accident aboard just before they reached land. Mail was slow to come, and frequently lost due to the war and the season. Miss Bingley—newly betrothed—and Mrs. Hurst gave him up for dead entirely. And in time, so did Jane.

Darcy and Elizabeth set up house at Pemberley; his sister joining them. Miss Bingley married at the end of the summer and became Mrs. Thacker, wife to a baronet's heir. Lydia and Kitty travelled to the Lakes with Mr. and Mrs. Gardiner. In their absence, Mary seemed to gain the notice of Mr. Griffin, Mr. Phillips' clerk, and Jane remained at Longbourn, where nothing seemed to change. As Michaelmas came and went, Bingley's lease on Netherfield lapsed and a new family took up residence.

Mr. and Mrs. Rutledge were a young and amiable couple with two daughters, six and four. Mrs. Rutledge was pleasant but did not add any sort of new quality to the Meryton society, which suited the other matrons admirably. She was friendly with Jane, which she appreciated, but they were not overly close. However, when she announced her widowed brother was coming for a visit in mid-November Jane clamped down on the urge to scream as her mother began antics reminiscent of Mr. Bingley's arrival the year before.

During one outburst by her mother, while Jane was trying to read a letter from Elizabeth, she could bear it no longer, even if no-one else seemed affected. Mr. Bennet had merely shrugged his shoulders and went to his library, not bothering to restrain his wife, while, Kitty and Lydia argued over ribbons and Mary sermonised on vanity and luxuries while awaiting Mr. Griffin's call.

"Put down that letter. Without Lizzy here I rely on you to arrange these flowers. Mr. Griffin may come any moment, and I will not tolerate one of my daughters losing a suitor again," Mrs. Bennet said to Jane.

She squeezed her eyes shut. She and Elizabeth always arranged the flowers together, but the truth was it was not an activity she enjoyed. She was held to the routine the family followed, and the task now fell to her. Regardless of her enjoyment she could scarcely look at a flower without missing her dearest sister and feeling untenable loneliness. There was no one left in the house who understood her at all.

"I am going for a walk," she declared, although no one seemed to notice. Retrieving her outerwear she set out with letter in hand.

It had been wet and windy lately but for once she did not care. She had always tried to take things in the best light but was hard pressed to find something positive in her current position. Mrs. Thacker and Mrs. Hurst had resumed their acquaintance with her—clearly they no longer saw her as a threat now that their brother was possibly dead and in any event uninterested in her as he had never attempted to see her the whole time his best friend was engaged to her sister. Her mother had not said it, even if her aunt had, but now that Charlotte Lucas was married, Jane was pitied and looked at as the next spinster in a making—all the worse because she was so beautiful that she should have caught a husband years ago.

She did not wish to catch a husband. She wanted a husband to catch her. Was it too much to ask for a gentleman to be so interested in her as to woo her? They all smiled at her, most of them able to carry on a pleasant conversation about the weather and cards but only one had truly tried to court her. It was her first year out, only a girl of fifteen, and eight years later she was exhausted and disappointed.

She would even say she was angry. She was not jealous, never jealous, but what were her options? How was she to feel when life moved on without her? Elizabeth begged for her to come and visit Pemberley, to even spend the Season with her in London. Jane knew if her mother found out she would be whisked away immediately, but Jane's pride revolted at the charity.

> Is it wrong for me to wish you find happiness of your own, dearest sister? You now have a very wealthy brother. There are no prospects for you in Hertfordshire, and it has been nearly a year since you last saw Mr. Bingley. Even if he lives, he does not deserve your faithfulness. Please, say you will come. I will be so lost this Season without my dear Jane…

A gust of wind blew the letter from her hands. Clutching her hat to her head, she raced to catch up with the wayward paper. Staring at the ground she did not watch where she was going and unexpectedly met with a solid wall, causing her to fall to the ground.

"Blast!"

Jane gasped at the curse. Looking up she saw a gentleman looming over her. He was average build, and his clothes showed him to be of some wealth, although she supposed him to care nothing for them. His great coat was spotted in mud, as were his well-made boots.

"Well, come on, girl." He stuck out his hand to help her up, and she meekly placed hers in his. His grip was strong, and he launched her to her feet.

"Are you hurt?"

She stared at him, dumbfounded. He was entirely unremarkable yet she felt as though she had met him before.

"I said, are you hurt?"

"No, that is, I do not believe so."

His lips twitched as though he desired to laugh at her. Unconsciously, her hands smoothed her skirt and then went to adjust her hat, only to realise that it was no longer on her head.

"I will retrieve your hat," he said gruffly.

Jane was confused by his mixture of gallantry and seeming indifference.

He brought it back right away, and she tied the blue ribbons under her chin.

"Thank you," she began but he startled.

"Eyes the blue of forget-me-nots under a midsummer sky," he said.

She furrowed her brow. The words seemed familiar. She must have read them in one of Elizabeth's poetry or botany books.

"Jane Bennet, all grown up," he remarked in something like awe.

"I do not believe we are acquainted, sir."

He shook his head. "Yes, I would assume the passage of eight years would erase all memory of me. I am Isaiah Burton."

Growing embarrassed as she could not recall him, she spoke hastily. "Mr. Burton, I am obliged to you. I apologise for delaying you. Good day." She turned to leave.

"You still do not recall me, do you?" He followed after her.

Bristling that this stranger would think she should recall him, she stuck her chin out. "As you say, if we have met, you acknowledge it has been many, many years. I simply cannot recall every gentleman of questionable breeding I meet with."

"With as many admirers you must have had, I am unsurprised. There was a time, however, when you visited your uncle in town when you did not find my breeding and manners so repulsive. Tell me, is that why you are still unwed? You did not correct me on your name, so I can only assume you are still single." His voice sounded a mixture of offence and humour.

She turned to face him and in her seldom-felt anger felt more like Elizabeth than herself. "Because I am three and twenty I must be foolish to not have flung myself on any of the stupid ninnies I have met with? Oh yes, marriage to any of them would have been a delight over my present state. For certainly being in the care of healthy and doting parents and living with my three younger sisters, must be very pitiable. Or do you presume marriage is the only tolerable position for a young lady? As you are so interested in my own state, I assume you are also unwed yourself. Now, why has not a lucky lady ensnared you, Mr. Burton? For surely your manner recommends yourself to all."

Having said her piece she turned to leave again. Her heart beat fast. She had never said something so unforgiving in her life. And she desired to flee before he had a moment to react. But was that...laughter? He was laughing at her!

"You have changed quite a bit, I see. The girl I knew was much too docile to have even a shred of the spunk for such a speech, even if you looked about as fearsome as a kitten. I shall have to amend my poem. You are no longer as mild as a lamb."

Her steps ceased as she recalled his words. Isaiah Burton was the man who wrote her very bad poetry when she was but fifteen. Her aunt and mother were certain he would offer for her, but he never declared himself before leaving for a business trip and before he returned she departed again for Longbourn. When she returned to London the following year she had not seen him, but was not so affected by him to even ask her uncle what happened to his business friend.

"Ah, so my words did leave an imprint." He said upon reaching her side.

My, was he smug! "Perhaps no girl could forget such lamentable poetry. But your triumph is premature, for it is you who seems to have not forgot me."

For the first time in her life, she fluttered her eyelashes like her youngest sister. He only laughed at her.

"That was a very good attempt but I can tell you have not used such tricks and artifice much since we last met. 'Tis a shame too, for few men could resist such impertinent words on a beautiful face."

She heaved a sigh. "If you will excuse me, Mr. Burton, I find this walk has exhausted me."

His face softened. "I did not mean to plague you, Miss Bennet. Please, you were enjoying your walk. The fault is mine, forgive me. I will leave you be for your solitary thoughts."

This was closer to the gentleman she recalled. One who made her feel as though she were his sole interest in the world.

"No, it is I who must beg forgiveness. I have been out of sorts lately. Your company is not obtrusive."

"Well," he said as he offered his arm, "I would be pleased to escort you home. Now, you mentioned only three younger sisters; I do hope no tragedy befell one. Although I do recall you mentioning one named Lizzy who was especially keen on borrowing your hair ribbons."

Jane smiled. "Oh heavens! I can hardly recall such times. You will be pleased to know that sisters can manage to become friends, even the dearest friends of all. It is Elizabeth who is no longer at home; she married in June."

She could see he did not know how to reply. Strangely, she realised she did not mind the delicate treatment from him. "I understand you are confused on how to reply. Lizzy is blissfully happy in Derbyshire, and I am happy for her."

"Of course you are. You always had the most generous heart."

"Thank you," she murmured. "Despite my earlier words about unmarried females having many options in life, there is little to say over how I have spent my last years. Surely with your business you have more to report."

"You do not wish to regale me with all the new stitches you have learned, the books you have read or the tables you have painted?"

She laughed. "I fear I am rather unaccomplished even after all these years! I still have no ability for music. I never seem to have the interesting observations of books like Lizzy does. With four younger sisters to add to the tables and fire screens in the house, I ceased such tasks early. I must sound obscenely silly and spoilt, devoid of any depth."

"No, you are refreshingly honest. But you must occupy your time somehow."

"I enjoy riding. Now that Lizzy is married I sit with my father a lot and seem to be the source of my mother's nerves."

"And before your sister married?"

They had reached the lane to Longbourn. "Here is home. Thank you for the escort." She furrowed her brows. "I never asked how you came to be here."

"My sister and brother-in-law have leased a home in this neighbourhood. I have come for a visit."

"Oh, then we will see you at the Rutledges' some time."

"Indeed." He raised her hand to his lips. "Very soon, I hope, Miss Bennet."

She blushed intensely before he released her hand. "Good day, Mr. Burton."

"Good day," he said before walking on.

Jane walked down the lane to her house, her emotions in tumult. It was only then that she recalled she never finished Elizabeth's letter. Perhaps she would reply positively to going to London after all.

When Jane announced to her family that she had met Mrs. Rutledge's brother, and he was already acquainted with her, she thought her mother would be pleased to have such early gossip. Upon remembering him as the young man who failed to offer for her eldest daughter in her first year out—which would have been quite the maternal triumph—she found him of no interest at all. Kitty and Lydia had not entirely recovered from their adoration of men in red coats, though Jane had hopes perhaps by Christmas the militia regiment which was quartered in Meryton could be forgot. Happy with the attentions of Mr. Griffin, Mary had no interest in Mr. Burton. So it was that a fortnight passed before Jane met with him again. Entering Netherfield with the knowledge that not only had Charles Bingley never loved her, but he was most likely dead, had been difficult for her in the past. Why it felt even more so on this occasion, she chose not to examine. Instead, she found solace in the fact that her mother had ceased her exclamations of joy that a new gentleman was in the area. Indeed, she bemoaned the fact that she could not decline the dinner invitation.

After dinner, when the men returned to the drawing room, Jane sat on a settee near the fire. She attempted to ignore the memories of a year past. The others engaged in lively conversation. Her mother's behaviour had not altered, but no longer were they met with sly looks of superiority. Mrs. Rutledge was as amiable as the master of Netherfield before her had been. Her husband could rival only Sir William Lucas in terms of geniality. She knew she ought to draw comfort in the fact that her family was accepted as equals, but somehow it all felt so rote and stifling.

"You are very quiet this evening, Miss Bennet," Mr. Burton said as he approached her side.

"I fear I have a slight headache." Her ache was lower, in her heart, but he need not know.

"I hope you do not take ill. I had expected to meet with you again earlier."

"I apologise, my mother has had many engagements in the past fortnight."

"And you no longer walk the lanes?"

Jane smiled a little. "No, I am not much given to walks."

"I recall you saying you enjoyed riding. Perhaps we could form a party some morning, and you might show me some of the best paths."

This gained a true smile from Jane. "I would like that." She had not ridden in many weeks. Now it seemed silly to deprive herself of one of the few comforts she had.

"It is decided, then. I will make all the arrangements and will call upon you when it is settled."

Although she knew he did not mean to call on her for romantic reasons, her stomach flipped. She had never had a gentleman declare something so plainly. "You must tell me more about your mount for me to ensure the best path."

A discussion on the temperaments of horses and their correlation to their masters then followed. Before bed Jane was surprised to admit to herself, she had never been so well entertained in the room before, even by Mr. Bingley.

A few days later she sat in the back drawing room with her sisters and mother, trimming a hat, when the housekeeper announced a caller for Miss Bennet.

"A caller! Jane, you have been so sly! Who is your admirer? Mr. Goulding is to inherit a nice fortune, and I know he has eyed you for the last two years at least. Well, make haste. Kitty you go along."

"Mrs. Hill, who is the gentleman?" Jane asked while her mother pushed her through the door.

"A Mr. Burton, ma'am."

"Mr. Burton! Well, what can he need Jane for? Kitty, you stay here. I will accompany Jane. The nerve of him to call without seeing all of us!"

Jane closed her eyes in mortification, knowing Mr. Burton could likely hear her mother as she ranted down the hallway.

Entering the room, Mrs. Bennet turned all sweetness. "Mr. Burton, so nice to see you again! How are Mr. and Mrs. Rutledge?"

"They are quite well."

"How nice of you to call on Jane. It was lucky for you that her other suitors have yet to arrive this morning."

Jane tried not to blush as Mr. Burton's face darkened.

"Well, I came to settle the points of a riding excursion Miss Bennet and I had planned. My brother and sister would like to join. I made mention of the plan with a few gentlemen the other evening, and I know the Misses Long also plan on coming. Do any of your sisters ride?"

"They do not, but we will have a merry party. Do you think it will be too cold for a picnic?" Jane felt her spirits lifting.

"Picnic! No, it is far too cold. You have such a delicate constitution, my dear. Indeed, I hate to even hear of you riding. We shall have refreshments back here, of course," Mrs. Bennet interrupted.

"Well, then it is all settled," Mr. Burton said tightly.

He did not stay much longer; Mrs. Bennet made easy conversation impossible, and Jane actually saw him go with regret. Surely it was only because she enjoyed the variance he added to their company.

The riding party was planned for three days hence.

"Why are you wearing your new ribbons, Jane?" Kitty asked as she came in Jane's bedchamber unbidden.

"Oh? Are they? I simply picked the first ones I saw."

"A waste of such pretty ribbons, if you ask me. They will have to sit under your hat."

"Of course," Jane agreed and Kitty stated her request to borrow a green pair of ribbons.

She would barely admit to herself that she dressed with more care than usual and picked these ribbons for they matched her clear blue eyes; or as Mr. Burton called them blue as a midsummer sky. Perhaps her hat would fall off again, or when she removed it while they took refreshments, he would complement her again. She was not vain, she told herself. It was not as though she wished for the compliments of everyone. He simply had more natural taste and a pleasant way of stating it.

She called out her farewell to her family, leaving before Mrs. Bennet could say a thing. She would meet the party on the path between Netherfield and Longbourn. When she arrived, however, she found Mr. Burton alone.

"Have the others fallen ill?" She asked with evident concern.

He looked nearly bashful with his reply. "I told you to meet us an hour earlier. I thought you would enjoy a carefree ride."

"I ought to say no; it would not be proper."

"Do you always do everything that is proper?"

She did, of course, but did not like the challenge in his tone. "No, I would be quite unbearable if it were so." She had never thought that but more than once she heard a jealous remark that it was unbearable she could be so perfect. She felt far from perfect.

"Then you will enjoy catching up with me," he called over his shoulder as he started off.

He was talented, there was no doubt, but Jane had been allowed to indulge her love and soon caught up with him. She was inexperienced with racing but could tell he allowed her to win in the end.

"How dishonourable of you, sir, to throw the race!" she exclaimed between laughs.

"No, it is the mark of a true gentleman to allow the lady to win."

Jane laughed again. "I cannot recall the last time I laughed so much!"

"Nor I. It must have been before Sophie died."

Jane could not place the name but then recalled that he was a widower. "Your wife. I am sorry for your loss."

"Thank you. It was nearly four years ago. It gets easier with time."

"Does it really?" she blurted out before she could think again.

He gave her a penetrating look. "You will think ill of me, but I have heard the gossip. I cannot say for you, but for me the pain is eased by the pleasant memories we shared. I try to remember those instead."

"Think only of the past as its remembrance gives you pleasure."

"Yes, exactly."

"It is Lizzy's favourite saying."

"It is a good one. I hope you will give yourself leave to remember the happy times, then."

"I shall try."

"No, you will succeed. You are made of much firmer stuff then you would allow most to believe."

"But you think you see it?"

"I always did. How many ladies would take care to notice the small and fragile blooms of forget-me-nots when there are lush rose bushes or orange water to distill?" He gave her a small smile, "Now, we need to return to meet the rest of our party."

"Of course." She followed him as they talked of the autumn scenery. For the first time in a year, she allowed herself to think of Charles Bingley with a modicum of contentment. He was a time in her life, an experience. It was over, but the beauty of it not forgotten. It was only time for the leaves of that period to fall away. A new season was beginning.

"Fitzwilliam," Elizabeth called out as she entered Pemberley's library.

"Yes, darling?" Darcy replied from his chair by the fire.

She approached his side and gave him a quick kiss. "I fear for Jane."

"She has promised to come to London with us."

"Yes, but her correspondence is taking longer. I worry Mother is being harsh on her."

"What does your mother say?"

"That we must rescue Jane from an unworthy suitor."

"What makes him unworthy?"

"He paid her attention years ago, and nothing came of it, but truthfully I think Mamma is upset that he comes from trade."

"Bingley's fortune comes from trade and presumably the gentleman was worthy when he first paid attention to Jane."

"That is not the same to Mamma; besides, she wishes for better now. She thinks Jane will make a splendid match due to your connections."

"Our connections, my dear," he corrected as he pulled her onto his lap. "Do you think Jane encourages his attentions?"

"I thought you believed her incapable of such."

"When I was an idiotic fool I did."

Elizabeth smiled. "We were both fools."

"Now, I think that if a Bennet lady is determined to gain a certain husband nothing will stop her."

"You make it sound as if I threw myself at you."

Beginning to nibble on her ear, he replied, "I would have dearly enjoyed that."

Elizabeth pushed him away. "Behave. We must be serious."

Darcy groaned a little. "So do you wish to retrieve Jane before Christmas?"

Elizabeth's eyes brightened, "Could we?" Then her face fell. "No, it is too much to journey back and forth and you wished to spend Christmas here."

"We shall invite your whole family here. We do not plan to go to London until nearly February. Jane will have a welcome respite from your mother before we go to town. She can make her wishes known about any matches then."

"Truly? My entire family here? It will not be too much for you?"

"I am certain your father and I will pass many hours hiding away in here or on the grounds."

"You wretched thing! Cast me off to deal with my silly relations alone!"

"Then we shall invite the Gardiners as well."

Elizabeth nodded her approval. "A lovely plan!"

Darcy leaned in close to her ear. "Elizabeth?"

"Yes?" she replied breathlessly.

"May we misbehave now?"

Elizabeth replied with a deep kiss.

Chapter 7

November 6, 1812

Jane awoke smiling. The sunshine promised a beautiful day to ride. Since riding with Mr. Burton nearly a month ago, she rode every morning the weather allowed. She sometimes saw him on a path and he would speak with her. Three days ago was one such day. It surprised her to see him with a small child on his lap. She had never heard anyone mention he had a daughter. Jane was happy he had such a nice reminder of his wife. The girl was named after her mother and was four years old. Little Sophie had bright brown eyes and thick brown hair. She reminded Jane of her sister Elizabeth. The two girls shared a certain mischievous air.

Jane also enjoyed seeing the evidence of Mr. Burton's affection for his daughter. If she were truthful she would admit her thoughts often turned to Mr. Burton, and as he had been in the neighbourhood for several weeks she could no longer claim it was simply the excitement of a renewed acquaintance.

The nature of her thoughts was less easy to decipher. She was accustomed to certain attention from the male sex. When she would direct her thoughts on the matter of matrimony, and the suitability of a gentleman as her partner for life, she found that she frequently could only consider how the gentlemen treated her and made her feel. She had painfully learned, through Mr. Bingley's behaviour, that such was no great revelation of their character. She still believed him the most amiable man she had ever met, but she could no longer admire him. His actions had proved him either fickle or capricious with her feelings. There was more to judge a man by than merely his manners. Perhaps that was what Elizabeth had been attempting to tell her months ago.

She was beginning to consider Mr. Burton as a gentleman of superior character. He was also becoming a dear friend, but she truly gave little thought upon if her feelings—or even his—ran deeper. Her mother watched him with hawk-like eyes but was not promoting the match; instead she seemed to dislike him. It was very pleasant to simply be Miss Bennet and not a paragon of beauty and virtue or to be judged by her merits as a potential wife.

About a mile from Longbourn she met with him again.

"Good day, Mr. Burton," she greeted him with a smile which he returned.

"Good day, Miss Bennet."

"Miss Burton did not accompany you today?"

"No, it is growing colder. She will come down to the stables and give June a carrot or apple though."

Jane laughed. "Forgive me, I do not mean to laugh at your horse's name."

"Sophie wanted to name her June after the month I brought her home in and I wished to name her Juniper. June was our compromise."

She smiled again. "My little cousins are persistent like that. They will have you compromise with them rather than be firm. I am certain my mother would say I am too lenient when I am with them."

"On the contrary, I am sure they benefit from your affection."

"Thank you, sir."

"I think Sophie will miss the countryside when we return to London."

"Oh? Will that be soon?" Jane felt uneasy at the thought.

"I am still settling affairs. It may be after Christmas."

"Mrs. Rutledge mentioned you will be moving to a new house. I imagine the memories of your wife may be bothersome."

He gave her a sad smile. "Actually, she died when Sophie was only a baby. We had been married just over a year. So, you see we continued in that home for quite some time."

"Forgive me, I did not mean to pry. I am sure it is painful to speak of her."

"Thank you, but it is well. Truthfully, it may not be as painful as you imagine."

"You did not love her?" She could hardly fathom the idea of him marrying without love.

"We were very fond of each other and our temperaments were well suited to each other. We were only acquainted for a few weeks before our marriage. I had decided to take a wife, and she was a fine candidate. She wished for a husband." He shrugged his shoulders, "Perhaps if she had lived longer it would have been more. I did and do miss her. When you know a person as a spouse, see them every day and begin to pass your life together, there ought to be a vacancy felt. I did not feel a very passionate love her, but I was committed to her. She was to be my present and my future; my whole life. It was strange, at first, to imagine a different course for my life."

Jane listened to him speak and thought she knew no gentleman more honourable. "Yet, you have made a different course for your life."

"I had to, for Sophie's sake."

"The poor dear, to have no mother," Jane muttered. She glanced to Mr. Burton to see if he had heard her and he caught her eye with a peculiar look in them. "I ought to turn back."

"Allow me to escort you."

He said such a thing nearly every time they met but now it seemed there was more weight behind the words.

Upon reaching the lane, she invited him for tea as it had been a cold morning. They were greeted in the breakfast room by Mrs. Bennet.

"Jane! What lovely news we have from Lizzy. We are all invited to Pemberley for Christmas!"

"Oh! How wonderful!" Jane had dearly missed her sister.

"I cannot wait to see my daughter as Mistress of Pemberley! Such jewels she must have! Such fine carriages! Mr. Darcy has offered to send two for us. His noble relatives shall visit as well." She glanced toward Mr. Burton, "Oh, do sit down, Mr. Burton."

He and Jane sat to enjoy breakfast as Mrs. Bennet chattered on. "Then you are to stay with them until they go on to London for the Season. I asked for her to take on Kitty or Lydia as well, but she would not."

"Mamma, what of Mary?"

"Oh, why had I not thought of that? Of course, Mary should go with you. Your beauty would shine all the more then."

Mary did not as much as look up from her book, but Jane felt for her all the same. Their mother meant well but frequently hurt her daughters by her careless lack of regard.

"Mary may enjoy visiting my aunt and uncle."

"Oh, of course. She would be no trouble to them."

Mary then peeped out from behind her book and gave Jane a grateful smile.

"We may be certain you will come back with a great match, Jane, for no matter how much Lizzy and your father say otherwise I am certain Mr. Darcy is still the proudest man in the world. He would not suffer to have anyone of inferior connections related to him."

Jane blushed at her mother's words. It was very improper for her to say such things in company about her son-in-law and Jane was now convinced Darcy was one of the very greatest of men. That Mrs. Bennet would choose to voice her complaints now, when usually she could not praise him enough, was a strangeness Jane could not puzzle out.

"How happy you must be at the thought of spending the Holidays with your daughter. When do you depart?" Mr. Burton asked.

"We leave in less than a week and we shall have to promptly host you and Mr. and Mrs. Rutledge for dinner, as I understand you will be gone when we have returned."

"Yes, I will shortly be returning to London." He paused and Jane saw him meet Mrs. Bennet's eyes. "In fact, my business associates were just begging for me to arrive with all haste. I ought to take my leave of your family now, for I may not be in the country for your dinner."

Jane was quite confused. He did not hint earlier at his departure being so imminent. In a matter of minutes, he had risen from his breakfast and said goodbye to the family. The whole thing was so strange. Jane knew not if she would see him again at all.

December 2, 1812

Despite fears that her family would overwhelm her husband and embarrass them both, Elizabeth greeted them in excitement. Only Jane seemed altered. Mr. Bennet was relieved to arrive at last and eagerly sought the direction of the library. Mrs. Bennet demanded a lengthy tour and quizzed her on the costs of every object. Kitty and Lydia were agog over Miss Darcy's gowns, entirely frightening the dear girl. Mary eyed the music room with covetousness. Jane seemed...content...or perhaps something more.

It was two whole days before she had a moment alone with her dearest sister, but she could resist no longer.

"We shall not be disturbed in here, dear Jane. This is Fitzwilliam and mine's private sitting room. Not even, Mrs. Reynolds will interrupt us here."

Jane blushed at her words. "Now, there is no need to be so missish. A sitting room is entirely proper."

If anything Jane turned redder and her eyes darted to the several connecting doors, clearly scandalised by even the hint of anything improper happening anywhere near their current room. She would tease no longer.

"How have you been? I worried when you began to delay your answers to my letters."

"Forgive me. I did not mean to cause you alarm! I found myself enjoying many pursuits and my dedication to letter writing was the price."

"Do not apologise. If you passed your time in happiness instead, then I am glad. Tell me of these pursuits. I am sorry you are visiting during the winter but if you stay through the spring with us you will get to see the beauty of Pemberley's grounds. I suppose you spent many hours in the still room?"

Jane gave Elizabeth an apologetic smile. "Actually, it was you who always desired to be walking amongst the flowers and forests." Elizabeth furrowed her brows and Jane hastened to reply. "I enjoyed working with you on the tasks you preferred, and I have terribly missed you but I now find great joy in riding every day."

How had she never known this of her sister? "Why did you never tell me? I would not have pushed my preferences on you!"

Jane grasped Elizabeth's hands. "I know, but you had very strong feelings on how you passed the time and I did not. I wished to have your company and offer you mine. I would not trade any of those hours with you but now that you are not at Longbourn it is necessary that I exert myself more to my own tastes."

"Dearest Jane! I had feared your temperament had changed due to your recent disappointments, but you are still as kind as ever!" Elizabeth squeezed Jane's hands and beamed with tears forming in her eyes. After a quiet moment, she cleared her throat and asked with a sly smile, "And were these solitary rides?" Perhaps she was more like her mother than she cared to admit.

"There was a riding party formed twice."

"You actually formed a riding party?" Jane was usually far too reserved for such a thing.

"No, Mr. Burton was the one who made all the arrangements."

"Mr. Burton is a relative of the new family that is leasing Netherfield, yes?"

"Yes, he is a very pleasant gentleman."

"Mamma was certain he was paying you attentions."

She crinkled her brow. "I cannot imagine what made her think so. He left Netherfield before even we did, and with barely a goodbye to us. The Misses Long were invited on our excursions as well as Mr. Goulding and Mr. Stevens."

Elizabeth turned her head to hide her smile. She immediately counted three couples, but her dear sister was as oblivious as ever to the intentions of men. She would guide her along this Season.

"I am glad the riding improved your spirits. You are welcome to any of the horses in our stables, of course."

"Thank you! It was not only the riding. I felt a burden lift. You know how melancholy I was after Mr. Bingley left Netherfield. I am now ready to face my future instead of regret the past."

"Excellent news! For I am certain once we have you dressed in the finest gowns of London you will be the envy of every lady."

Jane blushed. "Lizzy, I do not know if I mean to ever marry. I would so very much like to be sought after for more than mere beauty."

"And so you shall! Everyone who meets you cannot help but see how sweet and serene you are. No man could ask for a better wife."

Jane smiled but not as brightly as Elizabeth intended. Then her mouth slipped into a seldom-seen teasing smirk. "I am certain at least your husband would disagree."

Elizabeth laughed. "Oh, yes. He is much better about thinking before speaking these days!"

The two laughed, and the sisters discussed unimportant things for the remainder of the morning.

About a week after the Bennets came to Pemberley, Darcy's relatives, except for Lady Catherine and Miss de Bourgh, arrived. Elizabeth was relieved and hoped the presence of the Countess would help quiet her mother. The gregariousness of the Colonel and jolly Earl could only help matters as well. The Viscount had been unable to attend the wedding, as he was needed last minute at his estate. His demeanour was unknown to Elizabeth but one she believed would be enjoyable to sketch.

James Fitzwilliam, Viscount Arlington, was a tall man with dark hair and warm brown eyes. He was recently elected as an MP for Yorkshire. While it was clear he enjoyed the charmed life of the heir to an earldom, he also had an air of responsibility and maturity about him. Elizabeth could see he was instantly taken with her sister Jane.

After dinner, Elizabeth opened the instrument, and Lady Matlock was performing while Arlington eagerly sat next to Jane. Elizabeth sitting on Jane's other side was able to hear their conversation.

Seeing only Mary and Georgiana browsing the music books, Arlington asked Jane, "Miss Bennet, do you not play?"

"No, my lord."

"Then you sing, of course."

"Truly, I cannot, my lord."

Clearly casting about for something positive to say he concluded, "I am certain you would have very good taste had you ever learned."

His words were so very reminiscent of Lady Catherine that Elizabeth resisted the urge to laugh.

Jane smiled at him. "I wonder how that can be predicted, sir."

The Viscount laughed. "You must have mercy on me, madam. I am attempting to compliment you."

"Perhaps it is your punishment for restricting yourself to only the normal modes of conversation."

"What do you propose we speak of?"

Jane hesitated, and Elizabeth felt compelled to assist her sister. "If it is too sensible to speak of music in the drawing room then we must instead speak of politics."

Jane sent Elizabeth a grateful look, and the Viscount managed to monopolise the conversation for some time on his experiences as an MP and his hopes for the future. Jane was the attentive listener, but surprised Elizabeth with some observations. Jane had always been intelligent and sensible but now she lost some of her reserve and voiced her opinions more readily. It was encouraging to see.

As the evening wore on he sometimes engaged others in conversation but continually returned to Jane's side. Elizabeth watched it all with trepidation as Jane's heart had been broken by Bingley's very similar behavior but worried about prematurely counseling her.

Three days later the Gardiners arrived. Mrs. Gardiner was even shrewder than Elizabeth. During supper her very first night at Pemberley, she drew Elizabeth aside.

"Lizzy, I mean to speak with you very seriously about Jane. What can the Viscount mean by paying her so much attention? Tell me she is taking care to guard her heart this time."

"My dear aunt," was her reply, "I am certain any relative of Mr. Darcy's is honourable."

"Such as any of his friends were?"

"You can hardly believe her to be in danger of falling in love so easily again."

"I can believe her tender heart as much ready to fall in love as she ever was with such an amiable and respectful man who shows her every attention."

"I do give her more credit than you do, but I will ask Mr. Darcy about his cousin and if we should put Jane on her guard."

"Well, I only hope they will not be much in company in London."

The evening soon concluded and before retiring for the night, Elizabeth spoke with her husband.

"Darling, Aunt Gardiner was alarmed at your cousin's attentions toward Jane."

"Why should she worry?"

"We do not wish for Jane to suffer another broken heart."

"I know I have said so before, but I truly do not think she is affected by him."

Although she agreed, Elizabeth was annoyed he felt capable of discerning her sister's emotions now after being so wrong before. "The topic at hand is if your cousin could have any intentions toward her."

"He has been careful to never be so attentive before." She frowned, and he added, "He told me he means to find a wife this Season."

"I assume your uncle would be pleased if his eldest son chose for love just as he wishes his younger one will?"

"She will be the future countess so her behaviour must be superior, but if you are concerned that Jane's standing in society would make them object, I do not believe so. Do not impute my previous arrogance to all of my relatives, dearest. You know since…" he trailed off for a moment, and Elizabeth saw him swallow as his throat tightened in emotion. "You know since Charles has gone, James and Richard are my closest friends."

Elizabeth nodded her head but made no reply. She did not like how Mr. Bingley treated her sister, but he had been an amiable friend to all he knew, especially to her dear husband. The wretched war made it so difficult to know anything

He interrupted her thoughts, "Nor should you scheme to unite, any more than you should scheme to divide. Now, come to bed."

She gave her husband an anxious smile. She would not scheme, but neither would she idly allow Jane's heart to be used badly. They would enjoy the Season. Jane would be allowed to attend as many parties as she wished, and she would be allowed to make her choice, not due to family pressures or lack of suitors or anything but her own wishes.

Their parents ought to have taken them to London years ago but at last Jane Bennet would be seen by Society.

April 12, 1813

Jane collapsed on the settee in the Darcys' London house. She was exhausted. Eleven weeks in London and she was looking forward to the respite Easter would allow. In years past, Darcy visited his aunt in Kent for Easter. Lady Catherine was unhappy with his marriage to Elizabeth, and while Elizabeth had encouraged the breach to be closed in recent months, they were not yet close enough for a visit. Instead, they would visit the Bennets at Longbourn. They were to leave tomorrow.

Christmas had passed quickly once the Gardiners arrived. Jane was thankful for the presence of her aunt, as the attentions of Viscount Arlington were growing tedious. He and the other Fitzwilliams returned to London before even Fifth Night as they planned to visit Lady Catherine in Kent before returning to London for Parliament's return to session. January passed slowly but idyllically at Pemberley for the Darcys and Jane. She had quickly fallen in love with the Derbyshire countryside and loathed to leave it for London.

Once in London it was an endless barrage of soirees, balls, theatre engagements and morning calls. She had suitors aplenty. Some had admired her throughout her debut in

London; others paid their attentions to other ladies given her lack of encouragement. Viscount Arlington, always civil to everyone, had a clear preference for her.

"Oh, Lizzy. I will be so glad to return to Hertfordshire. Would you mind terribly if I stay there after Easter?"

Elizabeth frowned. "You do not wish to finish the Season?"

"What would be the point? I am exhausted."

"No one has caught your eye?"

"My eye, perhaps. There is so much more to making a match than a few pleasant conversations, I understand that now. How am I to know their character in only a few weeks on usual civilities in the company of so many others?"

Elizabeth's face took on a dreamy countenance. "Yes...something like long walks with talks on serious matters would be a better form of courtship." She shook her head. "If you truly wish to stay at Longbourn, of course you can, dear. But let us return for a week before you decide. In the meantime, should you decide you enjoy someone's company you know I will do everything in my power to assist you."

"Thank you," Jane said as she rose before leaving for her chambers. Alone in her room, however, she began to concede a fact she hoped never to admit. Perhaps someone had caught her eye already. Someone she experienced long and serious conversations with. And she let the opportunity pass her by.

Mrs. Bennet met her two eldest daughters with enthusiasm. Kitty and Lydia flocked to Jane. Darcy and Elizabeth shared a smile before he followed Mr. Bennet to the library.

"Have you had any flirtations?" Lydia asked.

"Flirtations!" Mary, who travelled with them from the Gardiners', scolded. "She should only entertain serious suitors."

"Suitors! I expected her to catch the Viscount by now!" Mrs. Bennet screeched.

"I think Miss Darcy would like to rest," Jane declared.

"Oh, certainly. She will share with you, Jane."

"Mamma, she can take the other guest room…" Elizabeth trailed off as her mother began to flutter her handkerchief in the air. She should have anticipated a mention of sharing her husband's bedchamber would cause such an attack.

"I would be delighted to share with Jane," Georgiana said, calming the situation.

Jane smiled. She really was quite fond of the young lady. She had once been concerned she held Mr. Bingley's affections but now she could only think that if he did return and meet with Georgiana again, they would be well suited, and their union would be blessed. Showing Georgiana to her old bedchamber made her smile. She could not recall the last time she thought of Mr. Bingley at all, and as it was she could only wish he still lived to ease the pain his family and friends felt at his loss.

As the days wore on at Longbourn, it became clear Jane could not stay and be happy. Her mother was already disappointed with her; she would never accept her decision to not return to London. Nor could Jane deny the excitement she felt when they called on Netherfield and Mr. Burton was discovered to have just arrived to visit.

"He came only this morning. He cannot stay long, and so Sophie remained at home." Mrs. Rutledge said to Jane.

Jane tried to show her surprise. "She is well, I trust?"

"Very, thank you." The man himself entered the room.

Jane turned to look at him and inhaled sharply. Had it truly been four months since she had seen him last?

"Mr. Burton," her mother said coldly. "We did not expect to see you again after your last visit when you left so suddenly. Few diligent men of business may have such freedom to come and go so frequently."

He gave her a tight smile. "I am sure you are correct. I am, fortunately, one of the few."

Mrs. Bennet was silenced for a minute, and Mrs. Rutledge joined in. "Isaiah, allow me to introduce Mrs. Bennet's second daughter, Mrs. Darcy."

"A pleasure, madam," he said and bowed.

"Mine as well. I have heard much about you from my family."

Jane felt her cheeks heat at Elizabeth's words. She could only mean from her. She dare not even look at Mr. Burton.

Mrs. Bennet cut in again, "Lizzy is lately married to Mr. Darcy of Pemberley, perhaps you have heard of him?"

"I think, perhaps..."

"He is nephew to the Earl of Matlock, of course. Jane has been with them since Christmas and experienced all the wonders of a London Season."

"How splendid for you, Miss Bennet," Mrs. Rutledge said.

Despite his lack clear lack of enthusiasm on the subject, his sister took it up with earnestness. All of Jane's attention was required for the remainder of the visit. She could only hope Mr. Burton still rode in the mornings but had no way of asking.

Happy was she when she found him the next morning. After the usual civilities, they talked of how they spent their time since their last meeting.

"I trust you have not neglected your riding since our last meeting," Mr. Burton said.

"No, Mr. Darcy allowed me access to his stables and I rode nearly daily. He was trying to teach Elizabeth, but she still does not have much patience, and little enthusiasm for such. But I often rode with Mr. Darcy and his sister."

"Did you ever have solitary rides?"

"Indeed, some of my favourite. Not that your company is taxing, sir."

"I envy you. The parks in town are certainly not as peaceful."

Jane frowned. "No, certainly not. Nothing in town is quiet. I confess I am extremely taken with Derbyshire, even more than Hertfordshire and certainly more than London."

Mr. Burton only smiled at the information. They discussed the variances of their travels. Jane had once visited a resort with her aunt and uncle. Mr. Burton talked of when he visited Jamaica for business shortly after they first met.

"It must be fascinating to see the different parts of the world. And you sailed too! I have never even seen the sea."

"You sound like quite the wanderer at heart, Miss Bennet. You enjoy the wild peaks of Derbyshire first, and now you wish to visit the sea."

She shrugged her shoulders. "My mother would say it is because I have a good disposition, but that would only make me content in life instead of thirst for new things, would it not?"

"I think I would agree."

"There once was a time when I thought I would always live near Longbourn, even after I married."

"Now you no longer wish to be close to family?"

She gave him a wry smile. "Some family may be better meant to visit. If I could settle anywhere, it would be near Elizabeth."

"Perhaps one day you may have your heart's desire."

She smiled brightly as her heart rate increased. "My heart's desire is only the love of an honourable gentleman."

He pulled his horse to a stop and earnestly met her eyes. "Miss Bennet, I…"

"Miss Bennet!"

Jane nearly unseated herself whirling at the unexpected voice. "Lord Arlington," she said in surprise.

"You are just the person I wished most to see. Everything was so dull at Lady Catherine's I thought I would call on Darcy."

Jane looked at the sky. "You will scarcely have a visit before you must leave for London again."

"Oh, I sent my carriage and valet ahead to the Inn."

Jane blinked. The Viscount would stay at their small inn? Worse, her mother would not allow it. Jane's eyes went wide as she considered just how her mother would rearrange the rooms to accommodate their newest guest.

In her silence, he had surveyed the area, and his eyes settled on Mr. Burton. "May I have the honour of being introduced to your friend?"

Growing more confused as the gentlemen watched each other she hastily made the introductions.

"Excuse us, Mr. Burton. Lord Arlington and I ought to return to Longbourn. I wish you a good day."

She saw his hold on the reins tighten, and June stamp her hooves from the tension. "Of course. Good day, Miss Bennet, Lord Arlington," he completed with a slight bow before turning toward Netherfield.

Jane could scarcely understand it all. Upon returning to the house, there was much fawning over the Viscount. The younger girls made themselves as ridiculous as ever before him, and Mrs. Bennet's machinations were patently clear to even Jane. She kept her fears to herself, but she was certain Georgiana was clever enough to see things for what they were.

The next morning she was, unexpectedly, the first to the breakfast room. Lord Arlington came down not soon after her.

"I trust you slept well, my lord?"

"Very. Which one of your sisters' room did I take?"

Jane blushed as she looked to her plate. "It is always a guest room, sir."

He smiled and then broke out into a low laugh. "I see what you are not telling me, Miss Bennet. For I am certain that room had been made up for someone before me. Well, I daresay my cousins have no complaints."

She nearly choked on her tea. Immediately he rose and came to her side.

"Take care, Miss Bennet, for I do not know what I would do without you."

Her eyes widened, but she could not cease coughing into her napkin.

"From the first moment I saw you, your beauty overtook me. It has been many months now that I have given you every attention. Your disposition and character are as delicate as your beauty. I am convinced you will be the perfect countess. I came just to see you; I had to see you."

Alarm was rising in her bosom but still she could barely speak. "Please, sir…"

"Allow me to finish, love." He knelt in front of her. "My heart has searched for many years to find a woman worthy, and it has loved none but you. My life will be blessed if only you will give me your hand."

Jane instantly saw he was quite sure of his acceptance, and indeed he had not truly asked. Memories of Elizabeth's offer of marriage from Mr. Collins in this very room came to her, and she began to laugh. She sincerely prayed Lord Arlington would take her refusal seriously.

"I know, dearest. I can scarce contain my joy as well." He joined in her laughter.

She did hate to pain him, but she must. "My lord, forgive me. First I cannot cease coughing, and then I break into laughter."

"I would wish you always so happy."

"If that is truly the case then you can feel no real remorse when I thank you for your kind offer but tell you I must refuse." She was rather amazed at the strength of her own words.

He immediately rocked back on his heels, entirely stunned. Rising, he asked, "May I ask why? Do you find our attachment too short?"

"The attachment you mention is not equal. It was never my wish to cause you to think so. My heart is attached to another."

"Yes, I have heard of him, but he is unworthy of you."

She rose from her seat in anger. "How dare you!"

"You have to put him behind you and move on. You live!"

She deflated and sat again. He had thought she meant Bingley. A terrible thought occurred to her, and she rose again.

"I am sorry, sir, that you feel you cannot accept my refusal. If you will excuse me…" she groaned as she heard a shriek from the direction of the door.

"Jane Bennet! You take it back! You will not throw your life away!" Mrs. Bennet came rushing toward them.

"My lord, please forgive her. She is usually of the sweetest disposition in the world. But he is nothing to her, nothing. I am certain she will not even remember him once he is gone away again."

"Again?" Lord Arlington asked in confusion.

"Her heart was touched by him years ago but it is nothing. Just the memory of a youthful infatuation."

Lord Arlington suddenly understood the matter and quickly excused himself.

"You stand right there and we will settle this matter with your father!" Mrs. Bennet shouted at her now least favourite daughter. "Mr. Bennet!" her shrill voice rang out again.

Darcy was the next to enter the room, wincing.

"Oh, Darcy! You must talk some sense into Jane. I see how you handle Lizzy, such a clever, intelligent man you are."

His lips twitched in amusement. "What am I to talk Jane into doing?"

"Why, marry your cousin, of course!"

He looked to Jane. "You have refused him?" She nodded her head. "I am unsurprised. I told Lizzy you did not care for him."

"He is a viscount! She can learn to care for him later," Mrs. Bennet rejoined.

"Pardon me, but I believe one ought to marry where the heart dictates and not according to wealth and rank. Such is the lesson I learned and followed and one that my family has wished for all its members to do as well."

Mrs. Bennet was silenced, but her anger continued. She fled the room, and Jane sat once more. Darcy brought her some tea.

"Jane, would you care to leave this afternoon?"

She numbly nodded her head.

"You are welcome to stay with us as long as you like."

"Thank you."

He twisted his signet ring for a moment. "Would you care to return directly to Pemberley? Or did you wish to go to London once more?"

Allowing herself a small smile she replied. "Yes, I would love returning to Pemberley above anything."

"I will inform Elizabeth and we shall make our plans, then."

He quickly left and before she could lose her resolve, she gathered her outdoor things and rode to Netherfield. She could not ask for an audience with Mr. Burton, of course, but she could visit with his sister and hope to send some kind of signal. At the door, she was told Mrs. Rutledge was ill, and the gentlemen had left at dawn for London. Sending her wishes to the mistress of the house she dejectedly returned to Longbourn. She could not alter their travel plans now. In any event, she had no hope of seeing Mr. Burton in London; their paths had not crossed in all the weeks before, and they had no common acquaintances. So, to Pemberley they would go.

Chapter 8

May 10, 1813

The wet spring weather slowed their travels, and it took five days to reach Pemberley instead of the usual three. As none of the party were the sort to talk incessantly, Jane had many hours to her own private thoughts. She left things undone with Mr. Burton. Their very conversation had been interrupted in a most untimely matter by the Viscount. As acquainted as she was with her own feelings now, she did not know Mr. Burton's. He may never return to Netherfield; it may be months before she was welcome at Longbourn again. They had no common acquaintances.

Despite this hopeless state, she did not feel gloom and despair. She was not the Jane Bennet from a year before. She would chart a new course.

Spring was making a vast difference at Pemberley and in the Derbyshire countryside. Jane continued to delight in daily rides. The estate was large and the nearest town miles away. Mr. Darcy always sent a groom to follow behind her, but Jane still relished in the freedom she felt. On a warm day in early May, she rode slowly into Lambton, the village near Pemberley. In the last fortnight, she had often travelled to the town, often with Elizabeth or Georgiana accompanying her. Today she shopped with only a groom. Her purchases would be small, and there was no need for the carriage.

Dismounting she smoothed her gown and straightened her hat then stopped still in shock. Only a few feet from her was the distinct outline of Isaiah Burton's frame. He was speaking with a townsperson who then nodded in her direction and Mr. Burton turned. Their eyes met. He acknowledged her and then made excuses to his companion. Her own legs carried her in his direction without thought. They met halfway.

"You are here," she breathed in astonishment.

"I am. I was sorry to miss you when I returned to Hertfordshire."

"And I you. We had to leave very suddenly. I tried calling on Mrs. Rutledge but she was ill, and it was explained you and your brother-in-law had gone to London."

"You have been at Pemberley since, then?" he asked hopefully.

"I have. Forgive me for the bluntness, but what brings you to Lambton?"

"I have bought Chester House. Do you know it?"

"I have not visited it, as I was here last during the winter, but I have been told it has a very pleasant park and…" she trailed off before anxiously meeting his eyes.

"What else have you heard?"

"That the elderly owner prided himself on his stables and riding grounds." She could scarcely breathe. Although logic pointed to the fact that he enjoyed riding her heart whispered he bought a house in Derbyshire but fifteen miles from Pemberley with room for horses for her.

"I hope you will be able to see it one day soon, Miss Bennet. It is lovely in the spring."

"I would like that. You must call on us at Pemberley."

"Indeed, I had planned on it. I only just arrived today to finalise matters."

"Then…we will look forward to your visit."

He held her eyes for a long moment before reaching for her gloved hand and raising it to his lips. "Good day, Miss Bennet."

After gathering her wits, she managed to nearly complete her small shopping list, forgetting only three of the four items she wished to buy and only one item bought by mistake being the most hideous colour of yellow. Upon arriving at Pemberley she eagerly sought out Elizabeth and explained it all. For two agonizing days, the ladies awaited Mr. Burton's call. When at last he arrived, Mr. Darcy showed him into the drawing room. The two seemed friendlier than Jane would expect upon a first meeting.

One by one Elizabeth managed to find some reason to have each person leave the room. At last Jane and Mr. Burton were alone. If she were not so nervous, she would have laughed at her sister's tactics, which were so reminiscent of her mother's.

"When did you say you mean to have your house fully set up?" she asked.

He smiled at her question. "In about a fortnight, however, it is not the done thing for a bachelor to host ladies. I dearly wished to plan another riding outing."

"Do you have no relative that might serve as mistress?"

"I know only one lady who will do." He had walked closer to her, and she was finding it hard to breathe. "You know I married without love years ago. When I resolved to move forward with my life, I also resolved to not remarry unless it was for a deep and constant love. I was intrigued by the young lady I knew many years ago, but the lady I currently know has so much more strength of character. I know you have grieved over love before, and I know we have had an interrupted courtship. I do not wish to leave things unsaid again. Might there be space for me in your heart?"

She took a steadying breath. "Indeed, you have my whole heart, sir."

They married on midsummer's day. The bride's gown complimented her eyes perfectly, as did the arrangements of forget-me-nots. Poetry better left unread by those of discerning taste was whispered in her ear.

There was no bridal tour as Burton was needed on business in Jamaica, the very reason he journeyed to London from Netherfield near Easter. Having had the love of her life absent more often than present, Jane refused to stay behind. Arguments for her safety were spurned. If they would die then at least, she would have her husband for what time remained to them. So it was in early July the new Mr. and Mrs. Burton and their four-year-old daughter left England.

A welcome breeze greeted the small family as they at last set foot on land again in early September. Their voyage had been as pleasant as such things could be expected to be on a vessel not made for passengers. The Atlantic was safe from conflicts with the Americans in the summer of '13 and as the Royal Navy enforced a strict convoy system with their merchant vessels they were saved the fear of being caught unawares by privateers. Hearing that the Americans were focusing on antagonizing British shipping off the coast of Chile allowed them time to complete their business.

After settling in their new house, Jane and Burton went out to meet with the silent business partner in his new venture.

"It is so beautiful and exotic here, but is it true the slaves suffer so much?" Jane asked her husband.

"Yes, and although Parliament has tried to implement provisions to lessen their burdens, the House of Assembly here resists."

"Are they very evil? I cannot imagine whipping and flogging a person."

"It is nothing more than fear that motivates them, dearest. The plantation owners are greatly outnumbered, and they worry if they are kinder then there will be revolts."

"Their money is so important to them?"

"I am sure it is, but perhaps some fear is justified. Not every revolt was as nice as the Americans'. The French people went through much less at the hands of their aristocracy, and we know how many of them lost their heads after the revolution."

"All the more reason to treat them kindly, or amend the system while they can."

"Very true, dearest. I do not know why you ever thought you were not intelligent."

Jane blushed. The only other person she knew who credited her with much sense was Elizabeth. Now away from the watchful eye of her mother she felt more at leave to read and her compassionate heart could not help but be touched by the lives of the slaves she read about in her husband's political tracts. Him bringing her along was a measure of how much he trusted her ability.

"What did you say the gentleman's name was?" she asked.

"It was not disclosed. This was to be very secret until the meeting. I only know that the others of the board found his recommendation very satisfactory. An elderly Irish baron, among others."

"Well, one hundred thousand pounds toward the publishing campaign would be worth the secrecy."

"Indeed."

Their carriage pulled up to a home very like the one they had rented and very shortly they were shown into the library.

"Mr. and Mrs. Isaiah Burton," the housekeeper announced.

A gentleman and young lady had their heads bent over the desk and looked up.

Two of the four immediately gasped, paled and blushed while the others looked at them in confusion.

"Come, sit, my dear," Burton said to Jane. "Pardon my manners, I fear my wife is unwell."

"I am well, only surprised. Nay, very astonished," Jane managed at last to explain.

"Yes, please do be seated," Charles Bingley said in a voice full of emotion.

"Tea will be coming presently. May I offer you some other refreshment, Mrs. Burton?" the red-headed young lady with him asked.

"Thank you, no…" Jane replied.

"Forgive me. It is a pleasure to meet you Mr. and…" he paused and looked strangely at Jane, "Mrs. Burton. I thank you for your forbearance in the secrecy of my name until now. I am Charles Bingley, and this is Miss Eileen Trench, niece of the Baron of Althone."

"Pleased to meet you," Burton and Miss Trench intoned simultaneously as Jane and Bingley stared at each other.

"Mr. Bingley, it would seem your presence rather than your identity was the shock to my wife," Burton said with some amount of distaste.

Bingley opened his mouth to speak, but Jane interrupted. "Mr. Bingley and I are acquainted. We met nearly two years ago when he leased Netherfield, in fact. It has been over a year since he was reported as likely dead."

"Dead!" the other three shouted in surprise.

"The only news your sisters or friend received of you in the last year, Mr. Bingley, was that your ship had been reported among those in conflict with the Americans. There were a number of losses reported."

Bingley closed his eyes at her words. "The journey was not an easy one. We did meet with the Americans. There was also an illness aboard and one particularly dreadful storm. It is not heroic at all for me to say that the most danger my life came into was slipping during the storm and spraining my ankle."

Jane stared at him in near disbelief.

Miss Trench must have sensed the tension. "I suspect the war has interrupted the mail. As the Americans have only just left for the Pacific, we are told, I think perhaps your latest mail may have reached England safely, Mr. Bingley."

Bingley looked intensely at Jane. "I did write; I have been writing, weekly. My penmanship is poor, and I have had to keep my interests here a secret, but I did write my family and Darcy. I hate to think how they have worried for me."

At Jane's silence, Miss Trench inferred the rest. "They do not worry; they mourn."

"Good God! Is it really true?"

"I am afraid so, sir. Nothing official was declared, but we were all quite convinced."

An uneasy silence pervaded the room. At last Miss Trench spoke again. "I am certain Mrs. Burton could tell you about your family."

"Oh, yes," Jane cried. "Mr. and Mrs. Hurst do well. They spend more time at his father's estate. Caroline married last summer to a Mr. Thacker, eldest son of Sir Joseph Thacker of Morris Hill You are expected to be an uncle by now."

"My word. And your family? Are they well?"

"Mary is betrothed to my uncle's clerk. Kitty and Lydia are still unmarried. Elizabeth wed Darcy last summer, as you know they planned."

"And you are happily married to Mr. Burton!" he said perhaps too cheerfully.

"Blissfully happy," Burton said and Jane sighed. His behaviour was reminiscent of when he felt threatened by Lord Arlington. It was clear to her he knew Bingley's name well from the gossip of Meryton.

"Mr. Burton's sister and brother-in-law leased Netherfield when yours expired," she provided.

"But my wife and I were first acquainted years ago," Burton added.

"We were," she gave him a smile. "So it was a pleasure to renew the acquaintance. However, as he was only visiting Hertfordshire and frequently had business to attend to, it was some time before we reached an understanding. We only married in late June, actually."

"My congratulations!" Miss Trench said excitedly.

"Oh, yes. Congratulations," Bingley said, perhaps in a more subdued tone.

"Thank you," Jane and Burton replied.

"And you have been very busy with business here?" Jane asked.

"Oh, yes. I arrived to consider sugar exports but upon seeing the conditions of the slaves and meeting with the Trenches, I scratched the whole idea. Miss Trench's brothers have convinced me to consider funding a new publishing endeavour. Naturally if the local owners knew of our scheme, we would be much disliked."

"You may catch more flies with honey than vinegar," Miss Trench added.

"May I assume by your presence, Miss Trench, that are you are integral to the order of the business?" Mr. Burton asked, and Jane was relieved they at last turned the conversation to business.

"Do not allow her to hide behind her brothers. It was her idea entirely," Bingley explained.

"Hush, you will embarrass me," she softly chided.

"Can I not praise my future bride?" he asked as he gazed lovingly at her.

Jane smiled. Indeed, she felt like laughing. Perhaps other ladies would be jealous as their former love bestowed attention on another before them. Other ladies would at least be regretful, but Jane now felt nothing but happiness. Since seeing Bingley, she first felt relief for his family's sake and then concern for his own heart as he was acting so peculiarly. She spared no thought to her own feelings; she knew them well. Her love for Bingley was nothing more than a candle in the darkness compared to the radiance of the sun she found in the love of her husband. Now, at last she could have true happiness.

August 1, 1838

Charles Bingley smiled at the guests in his old friend Darcy's dining room. Four and twenty years had passed since he set foot in England a changed man, one determined to end the slavery he witnessed in Jamaica. As of today, the first of August 1838, all slaves in the British West Indies were now free.

He looked to his friends and brothers in arms for the cause. Their dispositions were each as different as a well ordered garden, but each had been invaluable in his life. Darcy, of course, eagerly threw in his money and influence upon his return. Bingley never doubted his friend would, and in fact he had an acquaintance with Burton for several years. Elizabeth had eased Darcy's spirits some and was a charming but no-nonsense lady advocating the cause and raising five children.

He looked next to his wife's eldest brother. When they met, he was the young heir to an impoverished barony. His eccentric uncle freed all the slaves on their sugar plantation, effectively bankrupting the family, but they were zealous in their beliefs. Frederick Trench was very much like himself, amiable to all. Bingley could not help but like the man then hoping for a position as a Member of Parliament. Now, in part thanks to Bingley's own fortune, the family had modest wealth and the newest Baron of Althone still served as an MP; as an Irish baron he could not serve in the House of Lords. He had also married Georgiana Darcy when she was twenty and he six and twenty and new to the House.

Bingley next glanced to Darcy's cousin, Lord Matlock, as his new title was. A quarter of a century ago he was only the heir. The Viscount then was a rising Whig MP and eager to lend his support. Shortly before the Bingleys and the Burtons returned to England Viscount Arlington surprised his family completely with a marriage to his cousin Anne, who had long claimed no desire to marry. As Lady Catherine became more retiring with age, her daughter's health improved. Anne soon proved she had her mother's spirit and was not to be trifled with. The newest Lady Matlock was as formidable as her predecessor. If her husband regretted the loss of his first choice, he soon found comfort in his assumption of Jane's own objection. An affection based on a much longer acquaintance with strong familial ties suited his temperament and needs in life better. What began as a mild fondness had grown into a fervent love.

Their goal was simple. Bingley and some other investors, including some with titles, would financially back a press which would publish about Parliamentary debates on slavery along with any interest story which could gain public support. Within ten years, they formed a true society with the support of political giants like William Wilberforce and Thomas Clarkson. In another ten years legislation passed to abolish slavery in measures, culminating in final emancipation on this day—two years ahead of the intended date.

The six and twenty years that had passed since he left England for distant shores had been spent raising awareness and funds necessary to compensate slave owners. He left England in bitterness of spirit. He felt his heart lost to a lady he at first was uncertain he loved and then later decided was unsuitable. By the time, he saw clearly that she was at least worth the risk to his standing in society, as shown by Darcy's marriage to her sister, he believed all hope was at an end. The very evening Darcy had spoken with Bingley about calling on Jane and Elizabeth, Bingley was brokenhearted to see Jane speaking with another gentleman at the theatre. Any remnants of hope that Jane had ever loved him disintegrated. He had left her months before and believed whatever pain lingered in his own heart was better left hoping it would extinguish rather than risk inflaming it by meeting her again. He set out for a business venture before Darcy's wedding precisely so he would not see Jane Bennet again.

Now, he looked to her She was, as her husband declared years ago, blissfully happy, a doting mother of four who spent her life supporting her husband, although he remained in trade and Mrs. Bennet could never quite approve. Her eldest daughter, from her husband's first marriage, had married a few years ago and was gratefully giving Jane grandchildren. Now, Jane's younger daughter was betrothed to Bingley's eldest son. Soon, they would all be family in the way they were always meant to be.

He looked lastly to his wife. These two women made him. Jane was brave enough to give him up, but Eileen was determined enough to fight for him when he arrived in Jamaica with a bruised body and battered heart. She made him a better man and, if not for her, his life would have been little worth living. Eileen showed him there was more to live and die for. That others suffered worse than he. She showed him he could make decisions for himself, that he ought not to shy away from a confrontation and that he should not leave matters undone, for in the course of six and twenty years it was exceedingly tempting to cast off his lofty visions and allow younger and seemingly abler men finish this all-important task.

"Speech! Speech!" the crowd cried, and the gentlemen deferred to him.

He stood, with not a wine glass in hand, but a tea cup. "I thank you all, the friends young and old who helped in this worthy endeavour. You saw beyond the shallow fickleness of our lives of luxury. You looked beyond selfishness and saw suffering. And while even I was tempted to paint everything in the best light, there comes a time when all mankind must stand for truth and righteousness. And now…" he took a sip, "I very much look forward to enjoying my first taste of sugar in over twenty years, and it harvested from entirely paid labour. My solicitor will bemoan my pocketbook and my wife will bemoan my health, but I will drink it in delight and know the dignity our friends and equals in the Indies now have in earning wages for their work."

He sipped again, and an applause broke out. He held up his hand. "But there is more work to do yet, my friends. Let us not leave our business undone. Tonight we celebrate and tomorrow we work."

The group murmured their agreement and smiled in return. As he sat, he wondered what next would become the business of his life.

The End

Acknowledgments

A special thank you goes to Jim and Rosie for their wonderful editing; to Eileen and Kathy for making sure I wasn't too tough on Bingley and Jane; to Sarah for all her work on the cover and layout.

Thank you to the countless other people of the JAFF community who have inspired and encouraged me.

I cannot express enough how impressed I am with the work of Peculiar World Designs for the book cover!

Last but not least I could never have written, let alone published, without the love and support of my beloved husband and babies!

About the Author

Rose Fairbanks has had a life-long passionate love of history and has been writing historical fiction since she was ten years old.

Twelve years ago she fell in love with Mr. Fitzwilliam Darcy. Previously rereading her favorite Austen novels several times a year, Rose discovered Jane Austen Fan Fiction due to pregnancy-induced insomnia. Several months later she began writing. The Gentleman's Impertinent Daughter is her first published work. Rose has a degree in history and hopes to one day finish her MA in Modern Europe and will focus on the Regency Era in Great Britain and produce historical fiction novels of the era. For now, she gets to satiate her love of research, Pride and Prejudice, reading and writing….and the only thing she has to sacrifice is sleep! She proudly admits to her Darcy obsession, addictions to reading, chocolate and sweet tea, is always in the mood for a good debate and dearly loves to laugh.

You can also connect with Rose on Facebook and Twitter, http://rosefairbanks.com

"The characterisation was also very good, my favourites being Darcy and Georgiana. There were some fun twists and slight changes to canon as well, which I really enjoyed."

~Sophie, Laughing with Lizzie

"Charmingly heartfelt, this Pride and Prejudice novella variation is a sweet romance about Darcy and Elizabeth learning to listen to and obey their hearts. Letters from the Heart is perfect for readers looking for something light, unique, and entertaining to read!"

~ Austenesque Reviews

For more information about books by Rose Fairbanks, visit: http://RoseFairbanks.com

---

Coming Soon: No Cause to Repine

When a simple accident is misinterpreted and threatens Elizabeth Bennet's reputation her fate seems sealed as Fitzwilliam Darcy's wife. While the bride is resigned, the gentleman could hardly be happier until betrayals and schemes threaten to entirely take the matter out of their hands.

Made in the USA
San Bernardino, CA
17 February 2016